Night to Dawn 38

Illustrators:
Marge Simon: pages 9, 35, 71, and 84
Teresa Jay: back cover
Chris Friend: pages 3, 27, 62, and 82
Sandy DeLuca: pages 15, 38, 67, and 93
Elizabeth Hattie Pierce-Collins: pages 18, 44, 92, and 101
Denny E. Marshall: pages 7, 56, 69, and 97
James Masters: pages 21, 50, 74, and 81

Night to Dawn No. 38, April, 2020, Copyright 2020 by Barbara Custer. All rights revert to individual author and artist after publication. ISSN # 1542-1430; ISBN: 978-1-937769-64-2
Night to Dawn is a semi-annual publication of fiction, poetry, artwork, articles, and review.
Orders, editorial, and queries: Barbara Custer, P. O. Box 643, Abington, PA 19001
Email: barbaracuster@hotmail.com or ntdsubmissions@gmail.com
PayPal orders: venus1021@juno.com.
Submissions: ntdsubmissions@gmail.com; Web: www.bloodredshadow.com

Pickings and Tidbits

Top of the balloon to ya'll! ☺

We are now heading toward the hazy days of Old Man Winter. In the meantime, I released Rod Marsden's *50 Dragons*. It depicts a society where everything appears heavenly, but is in fact, monstrous. The story seeks to entertain, but you'll get a sense of which way our society is heading. His short story, "Reg 25," portrays a people overrun by Globalists, where getting old is considered a capital crime. The sequel, *Dragon Queen*, will be coming out in the fall, with more of the same theme.

For *Night to Dawn 38*, I've gotten contributions from artists James Masters, Teresa Jay (back cover), Sandy DeLuca, Marge Simon, Denny E. Marshall, Elizabeth Hattie Pierce, and Chris Friend. If you're looking for chills, Marge Simon provides that with her flash pieces, "Little Sweetie" and "Uncle Edward's Affair," along with her poetry. Each one comes with her illustration. To set the mood for the upcoming election in November, you'll want to read David Ennocenti's "Blood on the Hill." It features blood drinkers on Capitol Hill, both literally and figuratively.

Lee Clark Zumpe's stories will delight any spook connoisseur. A science-fiction tale, "On the Eve of the Battle," contains many horrific elements. It portrays the night Earth becomes a target for hostile alien forces. In "Dance Before You Go," Tristan gets into bad stuff during the war. When he returns home, he undergoes mysterious changes, and the women with him turn up dead. The narrator of "The Scourge of Zarablaan" leads his soldiers to take over a city. He returns home with a precious gem and a deadly plague. In "Centennial," a town gears up for a parade to celebrate its 100th birthday. Instead, its dark history interferes, and mysterious shadowmen have other plans for the people.

In addition to his poetry, Matthew Wilson delights us with two flash tales. "The Break In" features two boys getting into more mischief than they expected. "The Sacrificial Girl" is told by a man who once loved a kind witch, but because of her, he's running for his life. S. M. Bidwell is back with her poem, "Ichabod … Ichabod … Ichabod," and her story, "The Wolf's Moon." Here, the townspeople dread wolves, never thinking there are more horrific things out there than wolves. Linda Barrett's "Will the Real Me Please Stand Up" features Cedric on a quest to rescue a woman from an alternate realm, but he gets a surprise when he confronts the king. Rajeev Bhargava's "Zuguh: Abomination from Hell" starts out with a mother grieving her stillborn children. Her preacher offers an infant he calls "Zuguh," but this is no ordinary infant. As the old saw goes, be careful what you wish for. Francis-Marie de Châtillon's "The Curious Case of the Bookshop in Brighton" involves two portraits that people would say are haunted.

I've introduced several authors to NTD in this issue. Ron J. Cruz gives an unsettling review on "Evergreen Terrace Apartments." Matias Travieso-Diaz's "The Satchel" belongs to the protag (narrator), who set fire to his home. He treats his child as if it is still alive, but it isn't quite. Colleen M. Farrelly introduced me to haibun with her two short pieces, "Captain's Log" and "Shadow in the Night." While they're SF tales, the dark overtones make them good fits for *Night to Dawn*.

For issue 39, I will have stories from Margaret L. Carter and Todd Hanks (I have poetry from him in this issue). I'm also pleased to welcome Keily Blair as an intern. She will help out with the editing, and one of her stories will appear in NTD 39.

Since Count Dracula's legendary time, vampires have roamed the collective imagination of the world lurking in the dark corners of the mind, skulking in shadows, ready to sink their teeth into the warm flesh of unsuspecting necks. Night to Dawn seeks to breathe new life into vampires, zombies, mummies, vampires, and other undead night stalkers. ~ *Barbara* ☺ ☺

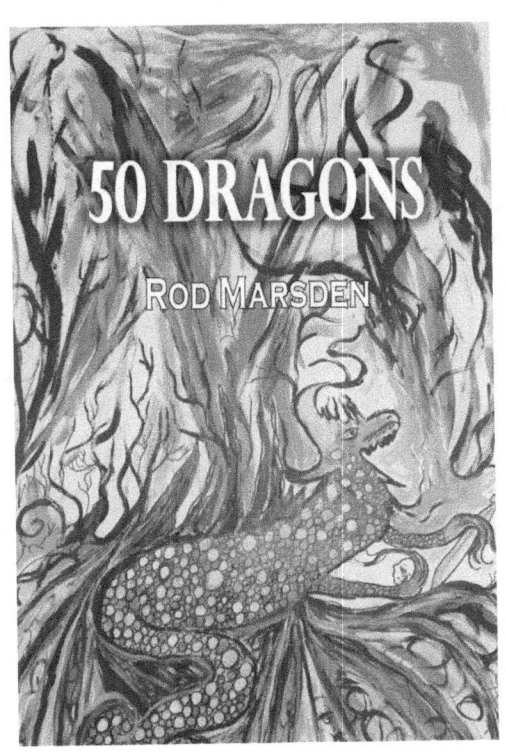

Peace meant sacrifice, and Dreadnought had already sacrificed so much of himself. He was scarred from battle and felt numb from his pain as well as that of others. Then one day, Dreadnought came to stare into the eyes of King Kamehameha and drew strength from him. Other knights would note this and also draw what they could from the statue of a long dead Hawaiian warrior. Amelia understood the angst Dreadnought felt as he got closer to his life goal. Would the High Ones allow this final victory and, if they did, what would happen to him and his love Amelia?

Available on Amazon, bn.com, and other major retailers!

On the Eve of the Battle
by
Lee Clark Zumpe

Starship destroyers lined up one after another, hovering just inside Saturn's orbit. Behind them, scattered across the outer reaches of the solar system, the remnants of a defense fleet drifted aimlessly in the dead of space. Earth had committed some of its finest forces to that sector, hoping to fend off an imposing invasion.

The deception of cunning admirals and the courage of combatants had proven no more effective than the tact of diplomats. Earth's outermost layer of armor had been penetrated, and the enemy had scarcely broken a sweat.

Sebastian counted their numbers, eyeing his instrument panel. Twenty-four alien ships lingered just above Saturn's rings, possibly searching the ice fields for small fighters that had limped away from the battle. Most of them, though, had managed to reach the base on Titan—most of them were safe … for the time being. The alien forces had not yet detected the small Planet Guard facility buried deep beneath the moon's surface.

It was only a matter of time.

"Did we even scratch them once? Did we do any damage at all?" A fighter pilot limped into Sebastian's control room. Sebastian, the station commander, glanced at one of his officers, then gestured toward the door. The officer left the room.

"Earth sent out seventy-two ships in all—forty-five cruisers, twenty battleships, and seven carriers. A minimum of five hundred fighters met their advance."

"How many did we lose?"

"I don't know. I know that all the carriers were destroyed—most of the cruisers and battleships are either gone or inoperable. I've only seen twenty fighters come through our facility. Our sensors detected a few others, but all of them had sustained heavy damages."

"And the aliens—how many did they lose?"

"Our weapons weren't completely ineffective…" Sebastian hesitated, glancing down at his monitors. His finger tapped the control panel. "We did some damage, according to the data I've reviewed…"

"How many," the fighter pilot pressed, leaning against the wall to support his spent frame. "How many of them did we take out?"

"None. We…" Sebastian shook his head, watching the alien ships moving across his screens. "We didn't do anything more than minor damage. We threw pebbles at tanks, shot rubber bands at armored columns."

Initially, Earth had been excited about making contact with an alien race that possessed comparable technology and seemed willing to barter scientific advancements as well as share thoughts on philosophy and theology. Early on, there had been optimistic connections between the two societies, and a cultural exchange commenced that seemed to benefit both parties.

For a decade, relations had been peaceful, friendly, and amicable. The aliens established a settlement on one of Jupiter's moons. They had reformatted the atmosphere and cosmology of the planetoid to suit their race. In a matter of months, they had adapted the moon and populated it with hundreds of thousands of their kind. Merchants, scientists, and entertainers all came to live in Earth's backyard to take part in the ostensibly innocent dialogue.

The aliens, though, had ulterior motives.

It became evident all too soon that their interests lay not in intellectual commerce but in substantial, material gains. Imperialistic in nature, the aliens had a history of colonizing new territories. They oppressed the indigenous peoples of their empires and drained their provinces of natural resources.

Earth became another target for their expansionism.

"So, the battle for Earth is over before it began." The fighter pilot slumped to the floor. Sebastian noticed that one of the twenty-four ships had broken off from their search pattern above the rings of Saturn. It slowly approached Titan, interested in the quiet moon--doubtlessly scanning the ball of rock and ice, hunting for traces of human habitation. "Do you think that they'll enslave people—I won't let them take me alive, you know … but my family…"

The station commander flipped a few switches and checked a few crucial screens. He reassured himself that nothing on the surface of the planet would give away their position. He cut power to the upper levels of the facility, locked down the core, and diverted power to the station's defense shields.

"My name's Sebastian…" He extended an arm and shook the pilot's hand.

"Kemper … Captain Corbin Kemper."

"I don't know what will happen on Earth. The aliens still have to face the Martian Defense Grid. That won't be a walk in the park…"

"No … but, it's not enough to stop them. We both know that."

"Our forces will fall back to Earth … and they'll put up a good fight. I understand that there is new weapons technology deployed on the moon. The aliens might find themselves outgunned should they manage to get that far."

"Commander … Sebastian … I don't mean to challenge you, but … well, let's just say that being a part of the Space Corps, I know what's waiting for them on the moon. And it won't do anything more than give them a black eye."

Sebastian's scanners indicated that the alien craft had put itself into orbit above Titan. Its sensors infiltrated the planet's surface, inspected every square inch of the planet bit by bit. Eventually, it would find the station—and when it had, it would use whatever firepower it had to eliminate it.

"Funny, you know," Sebastian mumbled. He fell back into a chair at the control console and unbuttoned the uppermost buttons on his uniform. "Our civilization went through this same kind of inclination. Strong nations subdued weaker ones—mined them for gold, diamonds, oil, food…"

"…and people…"

"Even after the empires dwindled and nations liberated themselves through revolution; even after the ideologies changed, and the industrialized world recognized their responsibility to impoverished lands—even then, the effects of colonization continued to hinder development."

"The stronger society always exploits the weaker one to grow stronger, and in doing so, weakens the exploited society that much more."

A warning light on the control panel told Sebastian that alien sensors had pierced the station's defenses. Sebastian closed his eyes and pressed his forehead into the palm of his hand.

"They've found us."

"We both knew they would."

"I have a duty to perform now … Earth fitted this station with a test version of their new weapon — the one they have positioned on the moon."

"The laser battery? The one they developed in the asteroid belt?"

"No … that was the cover story. This is something bigger … something different."

Sebastian used a set of keys to reveal a hidden panel on the console. He entered a code on a keypad mindlessly, then traced the outline of a button while wiping sweat from his brow.

"We can't allow that to happen to the Earth, can we? We can't allow people to be used like tools so that an alien race can increase its profits and spread its influence even deeper in space."

"What will happen when you press that button?"

"We can't let ourselves become cogs in some faceless machine." Sebastian pressed the button. The lights dimmed immediately, and all the computers and sensors and support systems inside the facility ground to a halt. The electronic defense shield, too, withered into dormancy. "Every bit of power has been redirected to a transmitter buried beneath the surface of this moon. It is sending a burst of energy — invisible, undetectable energy — speeding through space toward the alien's colony on Jupiter's moon. When it reaches that moon, it will locate a receiver placed there years ago; and upon picking up the message carried on that beam of energy, that receiver will set off a chain reaction that will tear that moon to pieces in a matter of minutes, killing every living being on its face."

"My God…"

"The radiation resulting from the transmission of this burst of energy is enough to kill us — enough to kill everyone in this facility. It would take days for us; it would be a slow and painful death. But the aliens will see to it that we die quickly now that our defenses are gone…"

"What if it only makes them vengeful … what if they don't stop their assault on Earth?"

"Then our forces on the moon will activate their energy burst … bathing both the moon and the Earth in radiation — and sending out a destruct message to a receiver hidden on the aliens' home world."

Sebastian and Corbin shuddered as the first explosions rocked the facility. The aliens had targeted the station and had begun hammering the surface of the moon with nuclear warheads. Lasers stabbed beneath the rocky crust and clawed at the uppermost levels.

In precious little time, the station had sustained grave damages. Corbin, eager to spend his final moments among his friends, parted ways with Sebastian in search of other fighter pilots. The Station Commander, alone, listened to his crew shouting as he shuffled down a corridor, waiting for the blow that would finish off the facility for good.

He noticed, though, a pause in the alien's attack — a distinct silence in their weapons. For a full minute, he waited, steeling himself against the coming barrage, ready for death, and confident.

He knew what had steadied the alien's hands. He knew what they had seen on their screens.

He knew Earth would be no colony.

The End

War of Vampires by Matthew Wilson

Ravens feasting on the dead
Unburnt bodies missed in the chaos
Making red-eyed birds lose their reflection.

Uncle Edward's Affair
by
Marge Simon

Uncle Edward's chair stands by the hearth awaiting his return, a folded Jewish newspaper, across its faded floral seat. The room's once paisley covered walls are water-stained and peeling like dead skin. Above the dust, a musky perfume lingers as if to mark Belle's passage.

Such a pretty thing she was, with silvery eyes and walnut hair beneath her parlor maid's white cap. Exchanging winks and blowing kisses, she'd lead him downstairs to her room.

What gaiety they shared in secret—all tickle-slap and pinch of flesh. Their muffled moans beneath the sheets—and not a one of us suspected at the time. The shame of it! Belle's specialty went further than a frolic in mid-afternoon. Alive, our Edward never realized that monster guised in loving bliss. Nor did he feel her fangs upon his throat. Within Belle's thrall, he drank her blood, which was her plan, his destiny.

Thus turned, he has eternity with her. But as for us, his relatives—she drained our lives away. We remain behind, mournful specters in this rotting manse. Suffice to say, we're not amused.

The End

The Traitor Prince Matthew Wilson

I have filed my fangs to stubs
I have thrown my caps upon the fire
To win the human girl's heart
A living soul who fills me with desire.

It was not I that killed her father
The tyrant king desired a war
He killed her hero father at dawn
And scattered his corpse upon the shore.

I shouldn't have freed her from prison
This troublemaker with eyes so rare
Thinking me a friend for saving her
Letting me run cold fingers through her hair.

I must use sunscreen against the sun
To dance with a human so fine of face
To never let her know my secret
That my tyrant father wished to kill her race.

"I'd love to get to know you better, John. But there's something you should know."

The Wolf Moon
by
S. M. Bidwell

"You shouldn't come here. I deliver so you don't *have* to come here."

Despite the hate shining out from the storekeeper's eyes, Diana remained calm as she replied. "If you didn't miss items from my list, especially when I've paid for them, I wouldn't have to." Her tone was mild, gentle. If something a little snide sneaked in, she could hardly be held accountable.

Old Man Carver gazed at her as if he would like to snatch up one of the sharp gardening implements which happened to be a turn and a pace within reach and use it to split her down the middle. Instead, he seized the list she placed on the counter, his teeth clamping together, his fingers bunching into fists. His tight grasp threatened to tear the paper as he scanned for the items she had underlined that he failed to deliver. His boots booming against the boards as he hurried to get the missing components were the only sound in the store, all else silent.

As one of the products turned out to be on a top shelf, soft curses followed, uttered under the man's breath but carried in the stillness. During this time, Diana kept her gaze forward, though her back was unprotected and vulnerable. Not that she believed the other women of the village possessed the courage to stab her, and the men… They would do other things before slicing her open. Those capable of murder did not regard the flesh as scared, not even the hidden, secret parts of a woman.

She hated their stares more than the thought of an attack. An assault she could react to, but there was no protection from the blaze of their glares. She shouldn't have come here, did so in part to torment these people with her presence. She survived almost entirely self-sufficient, but winter months were hard, and a few exchanged her preserves for coin to bolster other provisions.

Minutes ticked by, the hush fragmented by whispers. The door creaked open, muzzling free expression. Diana became aware of a considerable presence, prodigious in stature, colossal in self-possession. The longing to look was almost too much for her, made more difficult by other people's reactions. The tide parted for the newcomer, even if that meant moving closer to her.

Carver faced a dilemma. He stopped in mid-flow on his way over. His gaze darted from the man standing in front of him to the end, where Diana stood controlling the urge to smirk. He compromised—shoved her goods into the hands of his helper, nodded to the new arrival, and hurried out back to get whatever the man came for. Diana took her time placing the items in her basket, although there were only two, and only the small sack of flour was cumbersome. As she turned to leave, she tried to make the act of lifting her head appear natural, the direction of her gaze an accident or coincidence.

See me.

By wish or bewitchment, he did. Man and woman gazed at each other. She saw blue eyes so bright as to illuminate the darkness like moonlight, a head of shaggy peppered hair, dark stubble along a strong jaw, and muscle. Hunter and hunted. Diana suppressed a shudder.

Without pause, she completed the turn and headed to the threshold. Remarks followed.

"Witch," one woman said, following up her pronouncement with spittle. Diana smirked at the thought of Carver having to wash the floor, ignored her, and enjoyed the woman's confusion.

"Those raised by wolves should stay in the wild," another said. Diana agreed and breathed, relieved, as the cold of the day held out its welcoming arms. She plunged into snow and freedom.

"Those raised by wolves should stay in the wild."

Gabe heard the remark and clamped down on his instincts. His hand itched to grab the knife on his belt and to slit a throat or two. A moment of confusion followed. The insult was not aimed at him, but at the woman just gone. He had no need of the pronouncement—recognized another outcast when he saw one. Hunter and hunted. He fought to stop his lips peeling back in a snarl. Better than a knife, he would use teeth.

He handed over coin instead of death and took the box of supplies Carver had set aside for him. His movements slowed at the last as he remembered how the woman had exited the store with quiet dignity. He'd be quiet, but preferred indignation to dignity. He didn't even have to try. He glowered. No one said a word. They flinched back as the light of his eyes fell on each of them. Child, woman, man. He smelled fear, and the scent made him salivate.

Gabe ditched his goods in the back of the cart and then climbed aboard. Before he flicked the reins, Carver followed him out of the store.

"There're wolves aboard."

He'd heard this before, his reply always the same. "I don't hunt... wolves."

Carver's face twisted into an ugly grimace. "Then what the fuck do ya hunt wid these traps o' yours?" He glared into the back of the cart, although everything there was covered with a tarpaulin.

Gabe turned his head and peered down, giving the man his stare.

"I. Don't. Hunt. Wolves."

The man wanted to argue, but wouldn't. Wouldn't dare. A quick twitch of the reins and horse and the cart surged forward, making Carver leap back so fast it was a wonder from where he got the label of "old man."

Directionless, nevertheless, Gabe covered distance as though aware of his destination. At the edge of town, he paused, taking a swig from his flask for the sake of anyone watching. He considered it ill-advised to let anyone realize he ever hesitated. When his gaze fell on footprints in the snow, Gabe knew where he would go.

The woman. Her limbs slim but well-muscled. Her breasts pert. Hair long and dark. Gaze penetrating. Her clothes too thin for the weather. Funny, he should have noted that last detail, but he had. She needed something warmer. Likely something in the cart was suitable.

This prey would be easy to hunt—he only needed to follow her tracks.

****

Diana's mother had called this a time of silence. Winter was a time to warm oneself by the fire, but a fire took her life, and Diana, young and alone, fled into the woods away from the men who ignited the flames. There, she had lived in other ways, and, when a human had taken her in, she built a new life on the remains of the old one, existing between two worlds.

After winter came spring, and now was the time she should be planning the changes for the months ahead, choosing now what to plant when the ground thawed. Use this time to decide what in her life must be reshaped.

Had the time come for her to take a mate?

Diana turned her gaze from the fire and stood, making her way over to the door. She unlatched the lock and peeked out, drawing her shawl about her. The wolves were loud tonight. They called out to her. *Run.*

"Not yet." The moon was full, but so was she. Ripe for change, something new. Her family waited for her, but each year they grew bolder, less afraid of man. Her scent confused them, and that wasn't a good thing. She endangered them; they endangered her.

Tonight, the danger was a sharp scent on the wind.

"Maybe species aren't supposed to cross."

She spoke softly, but at the soft sound of her voice, he stepped out of the darkness, a shadow detaching from so many others, as she had known he would. She didn't flinch, start, or gasp, simply asked, "Where is your horse?"

He stared at her, glittering pinpoints sparking in his gaze as the moonlight shone down on him. He tossed her the gesture of down the lane with a jerk of his head.

"Best stable him." The jut of her jaw indicated the barn before she went into the house. While she waited, she made hot drinks, stoked the fire, pulled baked bread from the heat. When he entered and closed the door behind him, she was ready to carve.

"How do you like your meat?"

"Bloody."

His challenge was hers to receive. They consumed the meal in silence, wiped red fluid, and grease from their lips. They exchanged names.

"Diana, the huntress." His expression as he said this was one of amusement yet full of wonder.

"Are you looking to hunt, or be hunted?"

"Tonight? Neither."

"Gabriel… the angel?" How could she resist teasing?

"Just Gabe," he growled at her. "I'm no angel."

"No." She agreed with him. Her next question made her pulse race, though she was unsure why. Anticipation and trepidation combined with excitement. "Are you looking for a woman?"

"I know nothing of women."

"I know everything of men."

"I know nothing of men."

"No. You know only of wolves."

As though she called them, they howled for her. Gabe closed his eyes, turned his head, listened. When he opened his eyes again, it was to stare at her.

"They howl in hunger. A lasting and bad winter lies ahead of us all."

The possibility made her want to wrap her arms about her.

Piercing blue shone out of all that darkness. Diana sipped her drink slowly, although long cold. He was sure, and she believed him. Now that he said it, she recognized what she felt in the air and took into her lungs earlier. Another six weeks, more likely eight, and harsh ones. She had prepared as best as she was able but knew not if it would be enough.

"You're a trapper."

This time Gabe snarled the deep sound rumbling out of his mouth.

"That was a question, not an accusation." The truth was, she could often catch her own meat, but her body was too frail to run wild in winter. Sometimes the wolves left offerings for her, but they often forgot or fought over the catch before leaving the remains on her doorstep. In times of famine, she could not guarantee the wild ones would help her. In desperation, they might forget their association with her, turn on their own. This male might be her answer. Survival. Food. Mate. Procreation. Someone to run with.

"I'm too wild for you," he said, for the first time surprising her. He met her gaze, nostrils flaring a little. "I can smell you."

Smell? Oh…

Diana forced her limbs to remain immobile. "No shame in arousal," she told him, refusing to flinch, to hide her natural inclinations.

"I did not say there was." He leaned forward, closer to the table, peering out from beneath his brow. "I could eat you."

Diana refused to react. He didn't mean to devour her. His promise excited her, and he evidently detected that, too.

"You're a virgin."

A statement, not a question, and no bemusement.

"By choice. And my mate will also be my decision."

He nodded like she said something wise.

"As it should be, but you should know all there is to know about the male you take to your bed."

****

The chill wind took her scent away from him, so he couldn't be sure she followed, but he refused to glance behind. He strode to the cart which he had left outside the barn. From out of the darkness, bright lights shone — the moon reacting to the pupils of his fellow beasts. Sometimes, his eyes reacted the same way, and he turned his head to stare at the female, hoping she spied the animal in his gaze … if she had, indeed, followed.

She was so close, Gabe started. He might have been embarrassed, and then angry because of the embarrassment, but her gaze quickly went to the reason he brought her out here.

"You've never hunted the wolves around here?"

He shook his head.

"They've asked for you to?"

His conversation with Carver came back to him. "Yes."

"What do you tell them?"

"I don't hunt wolves."

"What do you hunt?"

He searched her face. No fear in her gaze, none in her scent either. "Evil." He pulled back the canvas.

Her lip curled. "You … eat these?"

"Only if desperation sets in. Only in times of dire need. The taste is not pleasant, but it can sustain." The truth revealed, what would she now think of him? Had he lost his one opportunity of finding a mate, or never had a chance?

Diana reached out, took a hunk of meat from the cart, and studied it. "I think… cooked, less bloody, I can disguise the flavor. We'd survive a harsh winter."

Still disbelieving his luck but unable to maintain his distance a moment longer, Gabe reached for her, lifted her smaller frame, hiking up her skirts. Her legs went around his waist, and he held her against him, hands cupping her buttocks. The wolves circled them, giving their blessing, but Gabe waited to see what Diana would do next.

She tossed the human hand back into the cart before kissing him.

The End

Ichabod ... Ichabod ... Ichabod... by S. M. Bidwell

A worthy wight by the name of Ichabod,
once tarried in the glen of Sleepy Hollow.
An area portent of Legend, the galloping Hessian
not least to chill the marrow of one's bones.
A tale told on winter evenings by the fire,
the haunting spirit of the Headless Horseman.

A pedagogue was Ichabod, not a tried and trusted horseman,
his steed corresponding with the figure of Ichabod;
an animal once broken, yet a spirit with some fire,
by the unlikely name of Gunpowder, looking hollow,
and starveling ribs, a rack of bones,
but with a gleaming eye to put one in mind of the Hessian.

Katrina Van Tassel dispels our schoolmaster's fear of the Hessian,
clouding Ichabod's dread of the Headless Horseman,
more concerned with the Herculean form of Brom Bones.
A formidable rival for one such as Ichabod
to contend with, though inside he is not hollow:
a yielding perseverance in his nature to stoke the fire.

So, it was one winter's evening by the fire,
when Dutch wives told tales to chill, the Hessian
Trooper's legend; the dominant spirit of Sleepy Hollow,
a glen not only haunted this night by the Horseman.
Not idle in limb or fibre, the swollen pride of Ichabod
dancing to win the heart of Katrina from Brom Bones.

Consider the indomitable figure of Brom Bones.
Brom Van Brunt, rustic hero, sweltering by the fire,
his eye set upon the clattering figure of Ichabod.
Burning with anger to match the wrath of the Hessian,
smitten with love and jealousy, his soul calling to the Horseman,
to search out a head this night in Sleepy Hollow.

It is the witching hour of midnight in Sleepy Hollow.
Ichabod trundles home, unaware of being followed by resurrected bones:
plump with thoughts of ripe Katrina, he is startled by the Horseman.
Gunpowder possessed as though by demon-fire,
the schoolmaster chased by the galloping Hessian,
by Wiley's swamp, a bridge over this stream, dashes Ichabod.

Rumours of the schoolmaster's survival in the Hollow are on fire.
Katrina conducted to the altar by Brom Bones; the Hessian's
legend, the Headless Horseman, spirited away, never to be seen again, Ichabod.

Will the Real Me Please Stand Up?
by
Linda Barrett

Cedric took a glass of champagne from the silver tray and an LSD sugar cube. He looked around at the other Harvard students.

"Are you sure this will open my mind for my philosophy thesis on man's inner nature?" he asked, lifting the sugar cube off of the paper doily.

"Anything to make Dr. Timothy Leary freak out in envy!" His friend Malachi laughed, retreating with the tray.

Cedric raised his goblet to the other 15 students.

"To the inner man!" he shouted before downing his cube with the champagne.

It took a while, but Cedric rode out the drug's anxious feelings. He sensed the flies buzzing Beethoven's violin concertos. His eyes studied the antique mirror across the room.

He heard a girl scream from within its tall, silvery form.

As he ran through the room's twisting and pulsating walls towards it, a gnarled tree stopped him by wrapping its branches around him.

"Watch that mirror!" it whispered. "You might break it!"

"I have to save that girl!" Cedric hollered, toppling the tree over.

****

Leaping into the mirror's baroque frame, he stood in an endless corridor. The walls seemed to breathe in and out like a human being. Doors upon doors flanked him. A Beatles song echoed down the hall. Cedric felt the floor vibrate under his feet.

The girl's scream came from his left. He sped on his champion runner's legs towards that direction. A door blocked his path. Cedric kicked it open.

A robed figure seated on an ornate throne stared out a window. His back faced Cedric.

"Who enters this place?" The seated figure intoned.

"Where is this place?" he shouted.

"Why should you ask?" the voice countered.

"I have to save that girl!" he yelled. "She's in danger."

"All women are in danger here!" the voice mocked him.

"Who rules here?"

"You must find out who he is," the voice challenged him.

The girl's scream compelled Cedric to close the door. He then opened one on his right.

A crowd of black-cloaked figures huddled over something atop a long table. The girl screamed from the midst of them, squirming against their grotesquely twisted hands. One of the figures raised a shining knife. Its corkscrew blade plunged into her shoulder. She fell backward onto the table, a stream of blood trickling down the open wound on her soft, pink flesh.

The knife-wielding monster prepared to stab again. Underneath the hood, the creature resembled a gruesome parody of Lyndon B. Johnson.

Cedric pulled a flaming torch from the wall.

"Get away from her!" he shouted.

They retreated. The girl sat up, her long red hair covering her nakedness. He knew her face

"Pandora Simms ... the Drama major." He raised his torch over her. He remembered having a crush on her, even if she acted aloof around him. "What are you doing here?"

"You are in his kingdom," she said. He helped her down.

"Whose kingdom?" he asked. She led him through the corridor. Statues of police officers beating civil rights workers flanked the wavering walls. Gilded framed paintings depicted U.S. soldiers setting fire to Vietnamese thatched-roof huts.

"The Unknown King," she said. "This is his realm."

Together, they traveled through a desolate land. Lynched figures hung from the tree branches like gruesome fruit. Their twisted faces resembled all the people he hated. Fountains of blood streamed down the vast castle's steps, spewing forth from heads of *Playboy* centerfolds. His nostrils took in the stench of rotting flesh. Heads of school teachers who reprimanded him were stuck on bloody pikes.

"I have to kill him to save you," he said.

"I'll take you to him!" Grabbing his arm, she pulled him along

She led him to the castle made of bones and torn human flesh. Out of the corner of his eye, he noticed that the body parts seemed to twitch.

At the cavernous doorway, she handed him a sword made from a long shard of broken mirror glass.

"It's the only thing to slay him." She gave him an open-mouthed kiss.

He found the King seated on the same throne, staring out the window. He turned around the black-robed figure wearing a skull mask.

"Kill me now and face who I really am," the King said.

Cedric thrust the sword into the King's chest. The mask's mouth spat out blood. He snatched it off.

A face stared back at him.

"Welcome to the real ruler of this kingdom," Cedric said to Cedric and laughed.

Cedric smashed the sword against the wall. It shattered into a million reflecting pieces.

The End

Kauket by Lee Clark Zumpe

Kauket nudged me from the edge of sleep,
her eyes encompassing
the cosmos –
she wanted to go skinny-dipping in the Nile
in the warm moonglow
beneath the shadow of pyramids
not yet commissioned
by pharaohs
not yet born;
reluctantly, I agreed –
and in her smile
I saw the arch of a new galaxy.

The Break In
by
Matthew Wilson

"I'm not going in there," Richard said, but his brother's mischief was up. "I don't think it works like that anyway."

Eric's total experience of vampires came from bad movies; but once a crazy idea entered his head, it was impossible to shoot down. "Just watch out for the zookeeper. I gotta get one of these guys to bite me."

"You'll have rabies before the power of flight, bro."

The bats screeched, annoyed as Eric crossed a string surrounding the enclosure marked DO NOT CROSS. Reading was for suckers, and though their Latin species name carried no syllable of vampirism, Eric had watched enough flicks to known he was on the right track.

He only had to be brave, get bitten, then he'd be the only undead in school. From a great height, he could drop terrible steaming things on his teachers who couldn't appreciate his greatness and marked his homework F-.

"This is bloody stupid," Richard moaned, carrying his own bite marks when he'd initially refused to help and the siblings had scrapped. Eric had always been a dirty fighter.

"Relax, just hold my legs while I hang upside down here and lift the latch."

"I'd need a bulldozer – how am I supposed to lift you, ya fat-"

"Hurry up, someone's coming."

Richard saw the flashlight before he heard the zookeeper hack spit as he wandered here for a crafty cigarette.

Busted.

"Eric, we gotta go."

"I'm almost there."

Richard had helped because he knew there were no such things as vampires, and while they were wasting an evening at the zoo, at least his damn brother wasn't stealing and pawning his cherished video games.

Now there was a chance of prison! No, he was too young. He'd be sent to juvie with other bad kids, and Mom would be so disappointed when she came to visit.

Oh, Richard. I thought you were the smart one.

"Eric, I'm serious, hurry."

Eric had always thought fast on his feet; it was the main reason the school nurse hadn't found that dead mouse in her car for two years. With a characteristic disregard for his own safety, Eric abandoned his plans to open the bats' cage and thrust his arm through the bars like a dumb gorilla reaching for a banana.

"Ow, damn it."

Richard yanked with all his puny might and pulled his brother free.

"Jesus, Eric! Your hand."

Eric held his blood-soaked hand up to the sodium electric lights and smiled. "Don't be jealous, but yeah, pretty rad, right?"

"Hey, you kids," someone yelled, and Eric pushed Richard out of the way. He'd never been good at math but had listed his dream job as uncaught criminal on things he'd like to be when older.

The door said "Emergency Exit," and like two drunks, the boys stumbled out into the rain.

"You idiot, we almost got caught."

"Almost." Eric savored the word and again inspected the puncture marks on his hand with great delight as if he expected them to eject gold coins at any moment.

"You're gonna have to have a tetanus shot before that thing becomes infected."

"God, all this running's making me hungry." Eric drooled. "Maybe I should start small, on something like a dog."

"Will you shut up – if you're a vampire, then use your power of flight to sneak us back through the bedroom window. Mom will have a fit if she knew what we were doing."

Fear of capture gave them wings, and the boys were home in no time, but Eric refused to go inside.

"You have to invite me in, stupid. Are you trying to get me killed?"

"This is your house, dummy." Richard said, too loud. Was Mom asleep or too worried to doze with her boys outside probably in a ditch somewhere? "You live here."

"Oh, no, you're not tricking me, human." Eric chuckled. "My vampire brain's a thousand times smarter than you."

"Well your vampire hand smells like cheese, so maybe you wanna wash it when you come in. I-I invite you."

"Thanks, man." Eric pushed Richard out the way again as he crept to the kitchen. Mom must have left some cold meat for supper.

Richard had had enough adventure for one night. He'd have the inevitable argument with Mom tomorrow – *You let Eric do what?*

Mom had always told Richard to brush his teeth before bed, but Richard feared it would make too much noise. He still had a bit of business to see to.

"Damn bats," he moaned when he snapped the bathroom light on. His thumb still throbbed. At first, he thought he'd caught it on the spikes covering the zoo bars; but when Richard removed his glove and saw the puncture mark, he knew that one of the little bloodsuckers had nipped him.

"Damn brothers," Richard moaned again, but stopped thinking when he reached for the paracetamol inside the medicine cabinet bolted on the bathroom wall.

He wondered why the mirror on its outer door refused to bounce back his reflection.

And why he was suddenly ravenous for meat.

The End

Bones of the Abbey by Matthew Wilson

From vessels of far north they came on evil winds
Howling men of bloodied axes to seek their fortunes
Killing monks for pleasure till the night destroyed the sun
Being a coward, I made it to the abbey's library first.

I was a monk in training, memorizing books to get ahead
I said the words on page 94 and lost my soul
Outside, the Vikings stopped cheering and screamed
When winged things tumbled out the torn stars.

Shrieking hate, the fanged creatures caught them
Twisting their fiery red heads off with their talons
None of the great warriors made it back to their boats
What limbs the creatures didn't eat they sported with.

Monks are good men on paths getting closer to God
Now I fear he has forever closed his gates to me
And I have to make a living since the abbey cast me out
Selling Viking axes at market to feed a body without a soul.

The Satchel
by
Matias Travieso-Diaz

There are two types of people in this world. People who hate clowns ... and clowns. D. J. MacHale

We have to be careful when we walk in the open. There are always bad people on the lookout for the likes of us, and if they catch us (as happened once, not long ago), there will be loud insults, kicking and punching, or worse.

The kids have been told to be wary of us, for we will try to lure them away for some evil purpose. They must run, and they must warn their elders so they can pursue us, cudgels and pitchforks at the ready. We are only safe by dropping back into the forest or reaching the foot of the mountain where there are sheltering caves. We need to avoid being seen during the day and only venture out at night to forage in the fields, catching small animals or plucking fruit from trees, and sometimes stealing eggs from hen houses. It is a miserable and dangerous life, made necessary by our own deeds and the cruelty of men.

It was not always like this. Before, I could stroll among crowds, hardly drawing attention from anyone. But of late, I needed to start wearing gloves and had to make a rough covering for my face out of thick canvas. We tried to make it more human-looking by stealing dyes from the tannery and turning the piece into a white oval over which we painted large smiling red lips, black eyes set below black eyebrows, and an orange ball for a nose. As my overflowing dark hair shot out behind and around the mask, the composite became the face of a jester, and not a good looking one.

Reflected on a rain puddle, the image of the mask was terrifying. We had an impulse to throw it away and start all over again. But there was no guarantee that a new mask would be less hideous, and at any rate, the mask was intended to conceal, not display my true self.

Now winter was approaching, and living off the land was getting increasingly difficult, so we had to move south to milder areas. A pass through the mountains was guarded by border patrols of two nations, but we managed to elude them in the dead of night, thanks to a violent storm that had the guards abandon their stations in search of shelter. The trip through the highlands past the border was arduous, with the cold winds cutting through our garments and food turning from scarce to non-existent. We nearly froze or starved to death until, by the grace of God, the last mountain pass was surmounted, and the land dropped gently to a much warmer region and where grasses grew and some fruits still hung from trees. We rushed down to find a respite from the cold and sample what the land had to offer; fish were found in abundance in gentle rivers, and field mice and squirrels were available for trapping and eating raw, for we hate fire and will eat nothing that requires us to cook it.

A few days after reaching the warmer region, we came to a hamlet where people seemed less violent than those across the mountains. We spied on the local inhabitants for a few days before deciding that it might be safe to approach them. Late one afternoon, as the sun started to drop behind the hills, we approached a hut that was set apart from the others and waved hello to an old man who sat on a bench at the hut's entrance. He was taken aback by our appearance, including the dirty rags that barely covered my body, the filthy cape, the large pilgrim satchel slung over one shoulder, the beard that protruded from below the mask, the frizzy hair, the gloves, and the mask itself. Even though startled, the old man waved back hello and made a summoning sign with his arm, inviting us – me and the satchel – to come closer.

Reluctantly, we did, even though friendly gestures are rare and need to be received with suspicion. The man began talking in an unknown language, but seeing that I did not understand, he mimicked a question. He rubbed his stomach and then pointed at us, asking if we were hungry. I nodded vigorously. The man got up, opened the hut's door, and beckoned us to follow.

Inside, it was all very rustic, plain wood table and chairs, earthenware pots and dishes, wildflowers in a blue glazed vase. There were framed religious prints on the walls and a small bookcase with dusty books on half-empty shelves. A faded yellow curtain on the back of the room seemed to lead to other rooms. On the stove, a pot of cooked polenta was slowly cooling. An old woman was bent over the counter, adding butter to a saucepan containing sautéed mushrooms. A jug of wine sat next to the saucepan.

The old man grabbed my arm and led us to the table. The woman took four wooden bowls out of a cupboard and ladled the semi-solid polenta into each of them. She set the bowls on the table, spooned the mushrooms over the polenta, and added grated cheese to each bowl. She did all of these with practiced ease, as the man filled glasses with wine.

I was focusing on the feast about to be served and did not notice that the back curtain had parted, and a young girl, no more than sixteen, had entered the room and approached the table. She uttered a piercing scream when she saw us and cowered, covering her face with her hands.

The old man and the woman rushed to the girl, seeking to calm her down. We became afraid of what might follow and took advantage of the momentary confusion to pick up a bowl, run to the front door, and disappear into the evening. Once a reasonable distance away from the hut, I savored the polenta, my first real meal in months. But we missed the warmth of human interaction, no longer to be had.

That night we sneaked into a sheep barn and, skirting the mildly protesting animals, found a quiet corner where to catch a few hours of sleep. Early the next morning, before daybreak, I stole a young lamb to be devoured later and ran away into the still darkened countryside as dogs started to bark their threats.

It took only a few days to determine that the people of the south were no different than those beyond the mountains. A few folks caught glimpses of us as we roamed the fields. They invariably shook their fists or made the sign of the cross. Once, we had to run away, pursued by a rainstorm of rocks.

After two months of fugitive life in this foreign land, we could not stand it any longer. We came upon a village and headed for the church, which was recognizable as the only building with more than one story. The wooden doors were closed, as it was well into the night. I pounded on them, demanding admittance. After a few minutes, a disheveled priest on a night robe opened the door partway and inquired:

"What brings you here at this late hour?"

"Father, I need to have you hear my confession."

"Can't it wait until the morning?"

"Please, father, I must unburden myself!"

The priest sighed and opened the door. "Come and sit for a few minutes while I get dressed."

A little later, I was kneeling at the confessional. "Bless me, Father, for I have sinned," I said.

"How long has it been since your last confession?"

"One and a half years, Father."

"What are your sins?"

"My sins are many, but I would start with the most serious ones. I have killed or caused the death of several people."

There was an audible gasp. "How did you do this?"

"My wife Coralina and I were mimes, traveling with a circus. Another mime, Domino, was also part of our act. Coralina gave birth to a beautiful girl with whom I fell in love right away. The afternoon of the child's first birthday, our circus was pitched on a clearing some distance away from a small town. Coralina asked me to go to the village to buy a torte and other goods to celebrate the occasion. I was halfway out on the route to town when I discovered that I had left the purse with my money behind. On returning to our tent to retrieve it, I heard noises inside, which were the sounds of love-making. I did not need to get in to learn that my wife and Domino were having intimate relations.

"I was seething with rage but restrained myself, partly because of deep shame at having to acknowledge Coralina's deception and also because Domino is much bigger than I and could hurt me badly if it came to a fight. I retreated to the ringmaster's tent and asked him to lend me some money, which I promised to repay before the day was out. The ringmaster was surprised by my request but gave me a few coins. So, I left for the village again, as a plot to avenge myself started to take shape in my head.

"My first stop was at the town chemist. I complained to him that I was having trouble getting to sleep and was looking for something strong to help me get the rest I needed. The chemist said this was a common affliction, and the best cure he knew of was valerian, which had been used for centuries to treat insomnia. He produced a copper tin full of brownish shavings of different sizes. 'This is ground valerian root, the best sleep-inducing agent,' he said. 'You can use it to make tea; a couple of cups of valerian root tea will put you to sleep in minutes. But beware: it has an unpleasant taste, like that of weeds mixed with dirt. I recommend that you add a lot of honey to the brew to mask the bad taste. As an alternative, you can use alcohol in any form, like wine, to dissolve the root slivers and disguise their flavor.'

"I thanked him and bought a pouch of the ground root. I then went to the wine merchant, from whom I bought a bottle of coarse red wine and a large flask. After leaving his shop, I emptied the entire pouch into the flask, filled it almost to the top with wine, and shook it thoroughly so that the ground root would dissolve. I took a small sip of the mixture: it tasted off, but one could think it was just the poor quality of the wine. I completed other purchases and returned to the circus as night was falling.

"That night, Coralina, Domino, and I had a modest feast with chicken, cold meats, fruits, and the birthday torte. As she served the dessert, I poured two generous cups of wine and handed them out. I gave myself a cup also but only pretended to drink it. Coralina made a face when she first sipped the wine, but before she could protest, I explained, 'It is wine from the foot of the Atlas Mountains. It takes a bit to get used to the taste, but believe me, it is quite good.' Domino let out a great guffaw and said, 'It tastes like the cheap wine it is, but I like it' and proceeded to drain his cup and presented it to me for a refill.

"Less than an hour later, the valerian had done its work. Domino was hunched over the table, snoring loudly. My wife had managed to stay sitting on her chair, her head sunk on her chest, also snoring.

"I took from my pilgrim satchel several lengths of rope that were part of the day's purchases and tied Domino's legs to his chair, and Coralina's to hers. The ropes would slow the lovers down for at least a few critical moments.

"I then glanced at the crib, where the baby lay quietly. What was I going to do with her? She was for sure Domino's child, not mine. All of a sudden, I hated her. Should she be spared? The answer was no.

"I proceeded to the last step in my revenge. I tore a sheet into pieces, soaked each piece in cooking oil, and set each on fire, tossing them into all corners of the tent, and ran out for safety as the flimsy structure started to go up in flames. I was only out a few steps when I heard the loud wail of a baby in distress. I had a sudden pang of conscience, rushed back into the burning tent, found her bellowing with her clothes on fire, and rushed out with her in my arms, screaming as the fire licked into my face and hands.

"Inside, Domino and Coralina had woken up. They tried to free themselves as the flames closed in on them. They failed, and their desperate screams resonated in the silence of the night. Help rushed in from the other tents, but the rescuers arrived too late.

"I ran until I reached the woods that surrounded the village. There I made a stop to rest for a moment. For the first time, I noticed that I was in great pain from burns over the exposed areas of my body. Turning to the child I held against my chest, I made another discovery: she was not breathing. I shook her tiny body, pinched her cheeks, tried to breathe life into her mouth. She was dead. I have no idea how, but she had perished in my arms, and it was all my fault.

"When my mind cleared somewhat from the pangs of pain and grief, I realized that I was the prime suspect for the deaths of Domino and Coralina, and it would not be long before they started chasing after me with riders and hunting dogs. So, we ran further into the wilderness. In time, I made this mask to cover my burned face, put on gloves to hide the burns on my hands, and went into hiding, always carrying with me the remains of my daughter. See?"

I opened the pilgrim satchel. Immediately, an intolerable stench of decay filled the small church. Peering inside, the priest saw a clutch of small bones, some with shreds of rotting meat attached to them. He convulsed and retched. After a while, he recovered enough to continue administering the sacrament.

"Your sins are grievous and call for retribution from God as well as man. You should surrender yourself to the authorities and abide by their judgment. As for…"

I interrupted, "But Father, I committed my crimes in another country. Justice would not be served if I am punished here."

The priest continued. "What to do about the justice of men is between them and you. As for the mercy of God, you must do a very demanding act of penitence."

"Like what?"

"Half an hour down the road that goes east out of town is a holding encircled by a tall fence. The fence has an entrance with a gate and a sign that reads "House of Lazarus." You must go to that gate and ring its bell, seeking admittance. When they come in response to the bell, tell them that you want to serve the community. They will let you in."

"What kind of a place is it?"

"A leper colony. What we call a lazar house."

"What if I refuse to go?"

"God will not grant you absolution for your grave sins without the required penitence."

I motioned towards the satchel, and we rose as if to leave. The priest watched as the satchel closed. He added, "And since this confession has not been completed and your sins have not been forgiven, I will feel obliged to tell the town's constable what you have told me and let him decide what to do with you."

I thought the priest was bluffing, and considered wringing his scrawny neck and bolting out of this accursed village. But we were tired. Very tired. So, I replied:

"Very well. I will go to the House of Lazarus."

The priest's face broke into a wan smile, and, raising his right hand, he intoned, "*Ego te absolvo a peccatis tuis in nomine Patris, et Filii, et Spiritus Sancti.* Amen. Go in peace and sin no more."

So it was that, as night gave way to dawn, the satchel and I found ourselves at the gate of the House of Lazarus. The bell, as I swung it, rang with great force filling the morning with metallic echoes. There was a long silence, and I was about to swing the cord again when slow steps sounded as an attendant approached the gate.

"How can we assist you, brother?" asked the attendant, a small, wizened man who seemed bent with age and fatigue. "I have come to serve the community" was my response, as directed. The old man sighed and produced an iron key, but before inserting it in the lock, he demanded, "You must remove your mask before entering this place. Here, nothing can be hidden, for the worst deformities of the lepers have to be observed and accepted without shame as God's will."

Those words lifted a heavy burden that had been weighing on my soul for months. I removed the clownish mask and let the morning breeze caress my scarred face. As the key turned into the lock and the gate slowly opened, I dropped the satchel in the woods behind me and walked in, seeking redemption.

"What was that?" asked the gatekeeper, noticing how I had discarded the satchel.

"Nothing much. The bones of a young lamb that I consumed a while back."

The End

Ghost of You Villanelle by Todd Hanks

I'll meet a faded ghost of you tonight
in shadows cast in Jenny Lincoln park.
I will not feel the slightest bit of fright.

We'll talk until the cruel and blatant light,
and we will hear the sound of singing larks.
I'll meet a faded ghost of you tonight.

Your death so young and pretty isn't right.
A death is cold and black as charcoal marks.
I will not feel the slightest bit of fright.
Your coffin black was narrow, hard, and tight.
A wild dog just dug you up with barks.
I'll meet a faded ghost of you tonight.
And now that you are freed from death's dark might,
you walk under the winter trees so stark.
I will not feel the slightest bit of fright.

You float above the grass so low and light,
where other couples kiss, embrace, and park.
I'll meet a faded ghost of you tonight.

Your form will always be a welcome sight.
It's pale and white beneath the rain-filled tarp.
I'll meet a faded ghost of you tonight.
I will not feel the slightest bit of fright.

Dance Before You Go
by
Lee Clark Zumpe

Floating, shoes scraping and shuffling on the beige tile.

Stewing, seething in the Barrelhouse, they coasted over the floor in concentric rings, not one meaningful embrace, not one clear-eyed offering of unselfish attraction. Cool jazz swirled like smoke; mugs chattered while they coughed up dry smiles and shallow laughter. Pale neon blue gleamed down through the oppressive mists, and the reddened tips of cigarettes bobbed like fireflies in the forest.

Drifting.

Her chin on his shoulder, his whiskers burned her cheek. Erin never asked him for a name. His improper smile, his dark eyes, his gravelly voice anesthetized her prudence. She paid no attention to the hand sliding down her back, stroking her hips with increasing vigor. He carried her, guided her – still, she was not altogether with him. She felt her lips part as he kissed her neck, there on the dance floor. The painted lids of her eyes sank, her fingers pressed against him. The music stopped.

She imagined dark maelstroms churning in his eyes.

Soon, the Barrelhouse was far behind her. Through the deep woods, the lights of the city slipped away apathetically. The sound of cars shambling home along the Foothills Parkway listlessly echoed through the balsams. Sirens mourned a suicide in the dark distance.

Ancient stars peered down upon her through the trembling branches, pine straw stabbed her neck, and dirt choked her. Unfamiliar whispers slithered into her mind, conspiring with the whiskey to distract her from the horrors at hand. She no longer recognized the man with the improper smile.

The scattered quasars and divergent clusters of celestial bodies seemed to melt into one brilliant light, and for a moment, the darkness cowered.

There was no pain, no feeling at all.

"Make it stop." The words curled across quivering lips, breath heavy with alcohol and fear. "Please, just make it stop."

****

Tristan winced slightly, reflexively, as the lukewarm tap water washed over his lips and tongue. He swallowed a mouthful. The aspirin stung on the way down. He set the glass squarely on the counter, but it rode along a puddle toward the edge and then stopped. The light spilling from the refrigerator played against the leaves nodding just outside the kitchen window of his mountain cabin. The darkness beyond engulfed the woods, the world.

Returning to his twin bed, feet dragging over the uneven oak floor and oilcloth rugs, his fingers tracing the paneled walls, he tried to chase the images from his head. The nightmarish visions hounded him no matter how far from sleep he retreated, coalescing over and over again. Spectral semblances became concrete forms, and ghosts from his dream manifested themselves in the shadows of the room.

He loathed the things he saw when he slept.

He fumbled for the stereo on the nightstand, hopeful but uncertain that music would drive them from his mind.

His fingers slid over the surface, finally discovering the play button.

Gershwin. *Rhapsody in Blue.*

As the night subsided, memories of his dream grew less perceptible.

Dawn brought patrol cars and vans filled with ravenous journalists eager for the opportunity to employ their pocket Roget's. Tristan stared blankly at the 14-inch black-and-white television reporting a breaking news story from the woods surrounding his home. The forest hummed with energy. Animals mimicked the frenzied disposition of the investigators and journalists. The dirt road leading up the side of Mount Richmond became clotted with traffic.

Another body had been found.

News anchors indicated that the cause of death had yet to be determined. As was traditional, this sentence was quickly followed by the familiar phrase, "but police aren't ruling out foul play." They might have been jumping to conclusions, but with the series of killings that year, it seemed a logical bit of speculation.

The morning's discovery brought the number of corpses found on Mount Richmond that fall to 17.

Tristan shuddered. He silenced the television and abandoned the Spartan living room, stepping out onto the wraparound porch and into the crisp Appalachian air. He could hear the commotion echoing through the forest, feel the sparkle of the mid-morning sun as it glimmered on the shiny white rooftops of police vehicles.

Had the victim screamed when she was being murdered, he surely would have heard her.

Feeling helpless and alone, Tristan eased himself into a wooden swing he had bought for his wife the previous spring. The sun continued to climb into the sky, and as shadows swept across the fern-heavy forest floor surrounding his cabin, he sipped chamomile tea.

Lisa would be calling soon.

****

A week earlier, the county coroner had packed up his belongings and headed for the sun-baked beaches of central Florida. Sixteen file folders had been stacked in a tray upon his desk, each one filled with photographs and half-completed forms and notes scribbled on sheets of legal pad paper. A tape recorder, used during autopsies, had served the distraught examiner as he sought to explain his resignation. In an uncharacteristically feeble voice, he stammered over contradictions and inconsistencies he could not explain. His statement was peppered with medical jargon, and each of these, he spat out almost resentfully. It seemed as though he was doing more than quitting his job and resigning from the field; it seemed as though he wanted to renounce his education and sever his ties with science.

Tristan knew the man well.

After his wife's murder, Tristan and Aaron became acquaintances – friends over the months. The fact that Aaron could not help investigators solve the serial killings weighed heavily upon him. Not one of the victims had offered up physical evidence that could lead to the killer. Not one had provided clues that could be substantiated.

Aaron could not even determine a cause of death.

Tristan had only asked about April once. Aaron responded, reluctantly, that it was as if someone had simply told his wife to stop living, and she had done so.

****

Cold, gray, dismal.

The day had deteriorated into a cowering shadow. Winter's footsteps resonated in the icy winds maligning the jagged ridge crests.

Lisa picked him up late that afternoon, smelling of discount store perfume and Mexican fast food.

A young journalist covering the story for the daily, Lisa had interviewed Tristan so often they had developed a comfortable friendship. Unlike her colleagues, she had treated Tristan compassionately from the beginning – never pressing him for details he could not share, never exploiting the awkward elements of the case, never once suggesting he played some role in his wife's murder. From the beginning, she agreed with the conclusion the police and the media had reached. Tristan was merely incapable of committing any of the crimes.

Together, they drove northeast through a haze of ghostly fog and gentle rain.

Someone had reported having seen the most recent victim at a roadhouse 20 miles down the Foothills Parkway around the fork that leads to Emmett's Cove. Tristan knew the place – old, dirty, seamy. It tied the latest victim to his wife. He called the police to remind them, but they had already connected the dots.

April had been cheating on him – Tristan admitted that to investigators months ago. His late wife met her lover at sordid watering holes in remote locations throughout the Southern Appalachians in the weeks before her death. She must have thought him too blind to recognize her infidelity, but he sensed it. Friends confirmed his suspicions, sighting her at least once on the dance floor at the Barrelhouse.

Tristan did not know the man's name. He cursed himself for not caring enough to confront her. He cursed himself for not caring enough. He had been so self-absorbed since coming home from the Middle East, he could not fault her for seeking some passion outside their detached, stale marriage.

"We're here," Lisa said. The afternoon skulked into the hollows behind the western range, and the purple murk of dusk loitered just east of the foothills. "You wanna wait, or come with?"

"No place for a woman to be by herself…"

"Great," she said, patting his hand, "You can buy a woman a drink, then." The reporter grabbed a notepad and pen from the backseat, handed Tristan his walking cane.

His blindness stemmed from an accident he had suffered overseas in the military – a subject he preferred not to discuss. During her first interview with him, Lisa – not realizing his condition – had voiced some tactless observation about wearing sunglasses at night. She still shuddered when she recalled her embarrassment.

"Anyone else around?"

"No, no cops anyway." The reporter checked her makeup in the rearview, batted her eyelashes, and shot herself a sensual smile that could charm a secret out of any man. She hated resorting to such tactics, but in this game, it proved essential some days. "Guess they've already cleared out."

"No one will remember – no one ever does."

Lisa had circled the car. She wrapped an arm around his, waited for him to get his balance. In those moments, she could see him surveying his surroundings. He breathed deep the Appalachian air, felt the wind blast him with sand from the dusty parking lot, and listened to all the subtle sounds that comprised a cacophony of which she was only vaguely aware. "They always remember the woman, but never the man."

"Maybe someone here will give us something." They sauntered along the wooden deck. The journalist took mental notes: Peanuts in barrels alongside benches decorated by pocketknife graffiti, burnt-out neon signs in the windows hovering over the corpses of flies trapped between glass and screen, squashed cigarettes doubled-over on the ground. "Maybe we'll find someone with a memory."

"What did the last guy say – he's faceless, featureless."

"The last guy also said he thought he'd been abducted by aliens." Lisa frowned as she opened the door. Inside, shadows, smoke, and bitterness gelled in a stagnant coupling. "We need to find a sober witness."

"They all say the same thing, though, Lisa." Tristan flinched at the stench polluting the filthy pub. Lisa paused as he tottered on the threshold, acclimatizing himself to the environment. She wondered if he could still sense faint echoes of April amidst the rotting timbers, the stained floor, the tainted upholstery. "It's more than a coincidence. It's like he can keep himself from registering on the conscious minds of others – like he can erase his image from people's heads. How is it that a person can have nothing distinguishing about him?"

Lisa led him across the dance floor of the Barrelhouse, dragging her feet lazily, allowing the fouled atmosphere to wash over her.

A man at the bar twisted his upper lip as they approached. He arbitrarily scrubbed mugs with a bar rag that appeared to fester with lime green mold and tobacco stains. He was alone, except for one lone cowboy slumped over the bar clasping an empty bottle of whiskey.

"Police already came in, asked their questions." Short and stocky, unshaven and terminally peeved, the bartender slapped the rag over his shoulder and glared at Tristan. "What's his problem?"

"I'm Lisa Nelson from the *Gazette*." She shrugged off the man's inquiry with flawless disregard. "And I'd like to ask you a few questions about last night's murder."

"You're a reporter?" The bartender's upper lip now twitched upward, forming a wicked sneer denoting some witticism forming in his putrefying brain. "Guess that makes him your photographer, huh?" Chuckling, he gazed at his solitary patron for encouragement but found him too absorbed in tonguing the whiskey bottle to acknowledge reality.

"Look, you're wasting your time," the bartender prodded a cigarette butt dying in an ashtray. "Nobody here is going to remember who they took home last night, let alone who left with that woman."

"Fine," Lisa said, nodding. "Well, how about a couple of beers, then."

Tristan and Lisa retired to a secluded booth in a shady corner of the bar. They loitered over a first and second round of drinks sedately, chatting as a host of local delinquents unraveled themselves from the Appalachian twilight. Lisa staggered her intake, not wanting to find herself even minutely impaired around the aberrant clientele the Barrelhouse attracted.

"You're sure this is the place?" Lisa could not picture Tristan's wife in a dive as disreputable as this. She knew he blamed himself for the affair, knew he had neglected her – but no self-respecting woman would want to end up in a place like this. If she had come here, she had been unfaithful long before his problems started. "I mean, it's just so…"

"Yeah. I knew a guy who spotted her here." Tristan's finger traced peculiar patterns in the condensation on the table – configurations that mimicked runes or Sanskrit, or some unidentifiable language. Lisa found herself trying to decipher the script. "It wouldn't surprise me if this is where they met the night she died."

"And you never said anything to her about it?"

"No. Not a word." Tristan ran his hand through his hair, rubbed his forehead. "This place is giving me a headache."

Before long, Tristan's head swam with a discomforting mix of drafts and sinister laughter. He felt the weight of memories pressing down on him, found himself repulsed by the ceaseless churn of depraved exchanges, the feigned flirtations, the offers of adulterous trysts destined to be consummated in cheap motel rooms or in backseats or remote woodland refuges.

Once, he thought he heard April's laughter, mocking him.

On the way home, Tristan dozed off in the passenger seat, unaccustomed to the effect of cheap domestic brew served in dirty mugs.

****

A State Trooper in the next county had his hands full at that moment.

"Step out of the vehicle, sir." Officer Bentley kept his gun on the subject while he eyed the shuddering tarp in the backseat of the car. He had heard something whimper beneath it. "Step out of the vehicle, put your hands on your head, and face away from me." The commands reverberated through the valley, made the cold mountains cringe. The Appalachians could discern the selfish ambitions of Death. "I'm not going to ask again, sir."

Distant sirens testified more officers had responded. Precious minutes separated Bentley from the backing of fellow law enforcement agents – and he still did not know the intentions of the man at the wheel who had failed to respond to every question, every demand, every word. He sat frozen, indifferent, expressionless, fingers gripping the dashboard, eyes closed.

For an instant, the man seemed ready to comply. He turned slowly, swung the door wide, put his feet on the ground. His hands dropped to his sides almost simultaneously, so gracefully, the officer paused.

"Hands where I can see them," he howled, an instant later than he should have.

The man's face lifted, and he grinned.

Officer Bentley saw no weapon. Later, he would tell a therapist it was like looking into the face of evil, like standing on the edge of a swirling vortex while a nagging, unfamiliar voice urges you to leap. He heard sounds he could not identify, saw silhouettes of nearby mountains waver and pulse against the fathomless chasm of the twilight.

Bentley fired three shots before he discharged his delusion and regained his composure.

****

Tristan grunted as he stirred from his nightmare, startling Lisa. She practically ran off the narrow road, twisting up through a tangle of rhododendrons on the side of Mount Richmond.

"Jesus," she said, standing on the brakes. "Are you all right?"

"Yeah, yeah," He swallowed back a wave of nausea, reached beneath his dark glasses to rub his eyes. In the incurable night that stretched out before him eternally, lingering images reached out from his receding dream to taunt and terrify him. "Bad one – nightmare. I'm sorry."

"It's okay, just scared me." Lisa drove another half mile and pulled into the dirt driveway alongside Tristan's cabin. Even knowing he was blind, she always found it disconcerting that his cabin remained interminably dark. When she visited him at night, she had to bring candles or a flashlight. "Still having the dreams – the same ones?"

"Yeah, the medication they gave me didn't help." He had told her bits and pieces about the nightmares that had been plaguing him since the incident in Iraq, told her about the intolerable clarity of the images, the grisly violence, the flowing blood, and the vivid scenes of death. He struggled to rationalize them as distorted amalgamations of both the atrocities he had witnessed in combat and the stories he had heard about the massacres that preceded him. Still, it never quite seemed to fit – not in his mind, anyway. "Sometimes," he whispered, "Sometimes it's like I'm forced to see through someone else's eyes – like my blindness opens a gateway on some level."

"They're just bad memories, Tristan." Lisa walked him up to the first step of the wraparound porch, gently placed his hand on the railing. "They're among the last visual memories you have, and your brain has unfortunately not let go of them after all these years."

"The last thing I saw," Tristan started, but he grew deathly silent, hesitating as he always did when he discussed that day. "The last thing I remember seeing – it was in Southern Iraq, we were looking for caches of weapons in underground bunkers. My unit found an abandoned shaft leading to an underground chamber – one not mentioned in our intel.

"Once we secured it, I was put in charge of the inspection. I found a little box – crudely made, and old. There was writing on the outside, carved into the wood." He remembered with uncanny lucidity those unintelligible symbols burned into his memory unlike anything else. "The box – well, the rest of the stuff in the chamber seemed to be looted antiquities – maybe taken from an archeological site before the war; maybe stolen from a museum in Baghdad.

"I should have left it alone. I should have inventoried everything, posted a guard, notified my command, and moved on." Tristan clawed at the memories as he recounted them, stammering from detail to detail, anguish contorting his face. "I should have sensed the danger – but I had to see what was inside the box."

"Come inside, Tristan." Lisa shivered in the cold Appalachian night. A sudden wisp of arctic air cascaded over Mount Richmond, coiling in the pitch-black basins and shadowy hollows. "I don't know if you should do this right now."

"Do you know what I saw in the box, Lisa?" The reporter pulled him toward the front door though he resisted. She plucked the house key out of a flowerpot, unlocked the cabin, and fidgeted for a light switch on the interior wall. "Do you know what I saw when I opened it? It couldn't have been there – galaxies sprinkled throughout great gulfs of nothingness, endless voids dusted with sparkling stars…"

"Tristan – you've always kept this part of your life a secret. I don't want you to tell me now because you've had a few beers." A fluorescent flickered in the living room, and the stereo in the entertainment center found a voice. Cool jazz and dim light flooded the cabin. "Let's call it a night, Tristan."

"No," he muttered, suddenly smiling – suddenly far from that hole in the ground in southern Iraq. She had never seen him smile, and his decadent expression served to both disquiet and mesmerize her simultaneously. She pulled away instinctively. "Wait, please," he begged in his gravelly voice. "Dance with me once before you go." The pianist urged her to submit. "It's been so long."

"Tristan," she felt herself blush as she tripped over excuses in her head. She felt his arms coil around her before she could speak, felt herself acquiesce. "Just for a minute, but I have to get home."

Minutes swelled into hours. Darkness blossomed in compounding waves, consuming each moment, eclipsing each whisper, smothering each uncertainty. She lost touch with the Tristan she had known all those months, found herself plunging willingly into an abyss, lured by something that only looked like Tristan – something distant and inaccessible, something unimaginable. His fingers traced mystic glyphs across her bare flesh, preparing her to be baptized beneath ancient stars peering through trembling branches.

In the forests clinging to the side of Mount Richmond, she found herself staring into his eyes for the first time. She lost herself to the dark maelstroms churning inside of them.

"Make it stop," the words bled from Tristan's shackled soul, crystallized and vanished in the icy Appalachian twilight. "Please, make it stop."

The End

Ripper's Street by Marge Simon

Softly settles East End fog,
thick with industry's residue.
It leaves an oily coat on the skin,
plays games with the vision.

Forms appear and vanish in the mist,
the stink of piss and rotten meat,
slimy creatures of dark alleyways,
these streets, the Ripper's playground.

Me being young, and with no binding ties
I went slumming with the lads,
begging favors of Miss Mary Ann,
we taking turns with her to satisfy

our bursting loins that certain night,
such was her service for our coins.
We bade good eventide and off she went
into that dense Whitechapel fog.

Years pass, and I'm a doctor now.
with a different take on whores --
they're still corrupting honest men,
giving them most dreadful maladies.

I walk these midnight streets alone,
carrying my own assorted tools.
There's many a strumpet up ahead,
for a trained man skillful with the blade.

Ullikummi by Lee Clark Zumpe

You with your pit-candle
chanting incantations
from some obsolescent lexicon
while the basement floor dissolves,
soul swallowed down the long
black throat of the earth
where the stone-god Ullikummi,
fossilized in mid-season,
poster boy for botched vengeance,
lingers amidst Milton's sights of woe,
where each word from your lips
is a pickaxe chipping granite.

Lover's Lament
by
Marc Shapiro

Cyril and Angelique were making love. She was lean, statuesque, big breasted with long flowing blonde hair. He was ruggedly European, well-muscled, and angular.

"It was like a romance novel cover come to life," thought Cyril as he nibbled at her neck while thrusting forcefully between her legs. "Even the canopy bed and the flickering candles seemed to fit."

Cyril looked intently into Angelique's eyes. They were lustful and loving in their intensity. "I love you," thought Cyril." But his eyes had long since passed the passion and heat. In their place was sadness and resignation.

"But I want to live."

Cyril's body was enraptured by the sexual heat and the vigor in which Angelique returned his lovemaking. But his mind had suddenly slipped a million miles away and a million lifetimes ago.

"So, I'll put aside those memories," he recalled with clarity as the images of the Euro-trash nightclub and how he had spotted her across the crowded dance floor flickered through his psyche. She looking uptown sophisticate and looking for...

"Of the night we met."

Locked together, our eyes exploring each other's souls. The sexual tension that could light up the night. The moment when I took her hand in mine.

"The look. The caress," remembered Cyril as their bodies continued their dance. "Driving through the night. The wind in our hair. The look of abandon on our faces. We were off into the place where lovers go."

A shuddering orgasm and Angelique's scream brought Cyril back to the present. And a lingering rush of physical pleasure that, just as quickly took him back...

"To the memories. The lovemaking on The Rhine. Dancing until dawn on a full moon Paris night. Sealing our bond with a kiss."

Cyril had hoped Angelique would be the one. And for a long time, she was.

But when you live forever, bonds grow ragged and brittle. You know when sex is all you have that you are truly the living dead...

"And I want to live," sighed Cyril roaring out his silent frustration as a tear streamed down his cheek. He moved his head slowly, tenderly toward Angelique's neck. In the past it had been the prelude to a kiss and so much more. But it was time to go their separate ways.

The fangs came out and eased into her jugular.

"So I'll cry as I taste your essence."

Cyril stood over her, eyeing the pleasure and the agony on his dead lover's face. He began to twist and turn, his own sense of being that came with the rush of blood sedation. His leathery wings unfurled. He was drawn, half-man, half-bat out into the dark. Sadness marked his monstrous face.

"And move off," the monster sighed as it moved to the open window, tasting the breeze as it looked off into the night. Its wings now at full span.

"Into another life."

Cyril looked back at the lifeless, bloody form of Angelique. The tears continued to flow as he moved silently through the window.

"And another love."

The End

Requiem for a Dead Bat by Marc Shapiro

The priest found the bat
Fluttering its last
Almost crucifix like
On the steps of the church
He bent over
Saw the signs in its eyes
In its spastic last moments
And knew that the bat had rabies
He knew it had been places
Flown the skies
And had experienced the horror and the blood
He knew because he had been in the life
In the night
And had drank his fill
The priest stared as the bat breathed its last
And disintegrated into dust
He knew what it was like to fight the impulses
The urges
And to be weak in the wake of it all
He knew that after the day's sermon
He would change with the coming of the dark
And once again drink
Perhaps to live
Or to die

Blood on the hill
by
David Ennocenti

"Asking a politician to give up a source of money is like asking Dracula to forsake blood." Cal Thomas

Senator Dramm slammed his fist on the podium. His face turned red. The jugular vein in his neck protruded.

"Bloodsuckers, all of them," he was reiterating his previous point. One he had made several times during this press conference.

Dramm was dressed in his usual manner: A gray pin-striped suit, white oxford cloth shirt with a button-down collar, and a maroon tie with a repeating diamond pattern. As always, he was impeccably groomed from his thick head of black hair to his wing-tip shoes. He looked much younger than his 56 years. He certainly looked more youthful than a man who had been elected to his fourth Senate term less than one year ago.

"I tell you greed is the reason for this constant gridlock here on the hill. Each one of my colleagues has one interest and one interest alone, themselves."

"Senator," a woman reporter intruded, "what compelled you to call this press conference at this time of night? Was it to call out your fellow Senators?"

"Does this have anything to do with B-2-S-A?" asked another woman reporter.

The Blood Supply Safety Act?" Asked Dramm.

"Yes," replied the same woman reporter. "Senator Osborne's bill."

"Well, yes, I have made it clear to Sheila that I am concerned about certain specifics in her bill."

"Just what could be wrong with a bill that makes the blood supply of the country safer?" asked the first woman reporter.

"Unintended consequences, we call that the folly of wanting A while rewarding B." Dramm continued. "The bill would make more testing necessary and put tougher controls on blood supplies. I fear it would reduce the available blood in the supply chain and make it more difficult for those in need to obtain blood. Nevertheless, the real reason I called this press conference is to announce my candidacy for President of the United States."

"This seems completely out of character for you," said a male reporter. "You've always been the low-profile type."

"Yes," said another woman reporter. "You've always stayed in the shadows, avoiding the limelight."

Dramm paused for a moment and reflected on her statement, thinking if she only knew how right she was.

"So," she continued, "why the sudden about-face?"

"I figure the only way to get anything useful done in this country is by having veto power, which only the President has."

"But Senator," the first woman reporter said, "Congress can override a veto."

"Only with a supermajority," responded Dramm.

"How do you intend to deal with that?" another male reporter asked.

"One step at a time," replied Dramm. "Thank you for coming."

****

Dramm took the Metro back to his colonial home in Georgetown. He reached into his refrigerator and grabbed a pint of O negative blood. He downed the pint in a matter of a few quick gulps. That long press conference kept him in need. The O negative hit the spot. Nothing better than the universal donor to quench the thirst.

He thought of that bill that passed in Congress. It was now on its way to the Senate. The bill annoyed Dramm enough to force him to throw his hat in the ring.

It's been said that as long as you're a Senator, you're always considered a possible candidate for President. Dramm, however, never considered the thought. He always felt that it would risk endangering his identity by bringing too much attention to himself. Being a Senator, even one in the shadows, was risky enough. The vampire community, however, needs representatives in all levels of society. Despite that, President was never on Dramm's list of possibilities.

****

"All right, let's get this meeting started," Dramm addressed the three Senators before him. They were meeting in a more obscure and isolated meeting room in the Capitol Building. There are many of these rooms scattered throughout the building. Insiders on Capitol Hill claim the public might be startled if they knew what went on behind those closed doors.

"Since yesterday when I announced my candidacy, all the press can say is, I'm a dark horse candidate. Then all of them buried it on page ten of their newspapers."

"That's *if* they published it at all," responded Senator Michael Mikelson, the Senior Senator from Minnesota, a stout man in his early fifties.

"True," said Dramm. "That could be good news. At least I won't be leading the news with bad publicity."

"If it was bad publicity, you can be sure it would lead," Senator Jenny Caparzo said. She was the Junior Senator from New Jersey. A brunette with olive-tone skin and much younger looking than her stated age of 47.

"Before we get started, let's discuss your problem with Senator Osborne's bill," Mikelson said.

"It's simple, as I've said before, the extra testing will make it more difficult to get our hands on blood."

"But the extra testing is for safety," replied Senator Ryan, a pretty blond woman in her early forties and the Junior Senator from California.

"Like hell, it is," answered Dramm. "Osborne's campaign donor is a company that will be hired to test the blood. That's the real purpose of the bill."

"There's always a reason behind the scenes for these bills, isn't there?" Senator Carparzo said.

"Yes, we all know that," said Dramm. "Think of the problems we'll have getting blood and keeping its disappearance a secret."

"He has a point," Mikelson rose from his chair as he emphasized his next point. "Do we want to go back to the old methods of getting our blood?"

"Hell, no," Ryan said. "I'm don't intend on hitting the streets late at night looking for a snack."

"I'm concerned about the dangers of reduced testing could cause," said Carparzo.

"What reduced testing?" asked Ryan.

"She's referring to my amendment to the bill," Dramm said. "I want the testing reduced. It's my way of making sure we have added ability to get to the blood supply. With less testing and fewer restrictions, there are more chances of getting the blood before an accurate count is made."

Carparzo slammed her palm on the table. "My concern is a failure to test for Van Helsing Factor."

Dram scoffed. "You're concerned about testing for a fictitious disease?"

40

"We don't know that it's fictitious," Caparzo replied. "Just because it's named after a character from the novel *Dracula*."

"Yes." Dramm laughed at her statement. "A fictional character and a vampire hunter." Dramm continued to laugh.

"And," Caparzo interrupted, "the archenemy of the fictional Count Dracula."

"Okay," Dramm continued his point, "we all know it's an urban legend in the vampire community."

"How do you know for sure it's just an urban legend?" asked Ryan.

Caparzo laughed. "He probably looked it up on the Internet."

The group laughed, including Dramm.

" Let's assume it's real," Dramm paused and raised his hand. "Why would humans test for a disorder that is not harmful to humans and is harmful only to vampires?"

Caparzo sat up straight to express her point. "Legend has it..." She paused to gather her thoughts.

"Well," said Dramm, growing impatient. "What does legend have?"

Caparzo continued, "Legend has it that some humans carry the Van Helsing Factor. It's not harmful to humans but fatal to vampires, and it tests positive as a simple contamination of the blood. So they dispose of it."

"That would explain why none of us has heard of a dead vampire from the blood supply," said Mikelson.

"That, and because maybe there is no such thing as Van Helsing Factor," said Ryan.

"Good point," added Dramm.

"One other thing," Caparzo continued, "They say when a vampire gets the blood, it burns, and the vampire dies an immediate death."

"That is *if* it were real," Dramm said. "Anything else to add, Caparzo?"

"Yes," she replied. "The legend has it that if a vampire bites into a carrier of Van Helsing Factor, they experience a strong burning and die immediately."

"Yes," Ryan interrupted. "You said that."

"And then," Caparzo continued, "the victim of the vampire lives on ... as a vampire."

"Enough of this nonsense," said Dramm. "We're getting off-topic."

"We're senators," said Mikelson. "What else is new?"

"Look," said Dramm. His voice got louder, and his pace quickened. "We need to focus on expanding our power base. Let's get back to that."

"You mean, get back to your Presidential ambitions," said Caparzo.

"Exactly," Dramm replied.

"Let's say you get elected," Ryan said. "You have veto power, but Congress can override a veto."

"Yes, but it's a big step towards the power we need," said Mikelson.

"We need to get more of our kind elected," said Senator Ryan.

"That's the problem," said Dramm. "You know how difficult it is to get one of us elected."

"That's because we only come out at night," said Mikelson.

"He's right," said Caparzo. "It was difficult even running for re-election last year even though my opponent ran a practically nonexistent campaign."

"How many more members would we need to veto-proof a bill?" Dramm asked.

"I'd estimate about eight," answered Mikelson.

"How many would we need to prevent overriding a veto if I'm elected?" asked Dramm.

"About the same," said Ryan.

"That's assuming the usual support we have from nonmembers," added Caparzo.

"And, depending on how the house is situated," said Mikelson.

"I think we need to consider alternative solutions in addition to getting more of us elected," said Dramm.

"Like what?" Ryan asked.

"Like turning other members of the Senate," replied Dramm.

"Are you crazy?" Caparzo stood and stared at Dramm.

"No, he's right," said Mikelson. "If we can turn some, we can bring them inside."

"You want to turn members of the United States Senate into vampires?" asked Ryan.

"Absolutely," replied Dramm. "Like he just said, we can bring them inside."

"What makes you so sure that they would come inside our circle?" Caparzo asked.

"Would they have a choice?" Dramm questioned.

"They would have to out of survival," said Ryan. "They would need the support of their kind. Party lines wouldn't matter at that point."

"I have to admit that's probably true," said Caparzo.

"What if the truth leaks out?" Mikelson asked.

"What if it does?" Dramm shrugged.

"It could ruin all of us," said Ryan.

"Look," said Dramm. "First of all, there's the possibility that no one would believe it. Even if they did, I would say only one-third of the constituents would care; the rest would be so apathetic as always and ignore the truth or go along with business as usual."

"He has a point," said Mikelson. "Even in an election year when everyone is screaming 'throw the bums out,' they always mean someone else's bum, and then they vote for the incumbent in their district."

"It would probably be the same even if their incumbent is a vampire," said Dramm. "Besides, we could be discovered at any time. It doesn't have to be because a member of the Senate was turned."

"True, but we don't need to force it," replied Caparzo.

"I say, we go ahead and start making plans," said Ryan.

"I agree," said Mikelson.

"Okay, I'll bite," said Caparzo.

"Hold that thought," said Dramm,

The group laughed.

"Good," said Dramm, "there are enough of us in the Senate now that if we add another eight or more after the elections next year, we can own the Senate."

"Yes, eight or more by electing new vampires and turning some incumbents," said Mikelson.

"Any ideas of how we start?" Caparzo asked.

A sly smile came over Dramm's face. "Well, since this isn't an election year, we won't be home campaigning, so I thought I'd host a Senate Halloween party." He paused and rubbed his hands together. "I'm going as Count Dracula."

****

Dramm's home was large enough for a large Halloween gathering. The wall-sized screen HDTV preoccupied about 20 guests in the living room. His den held another 20 who were listening to Bach's *Brandenburg Concertos* on the surround sound stereo system. Another 20 had scattered throughout the rest of the house.

Sheila Osborn, the senior Senator from Maryland, was in the kitchen enjoying a glass of Domaine Romanee' Conti Richebourg. She had dressed as Little Red Riding Hood. Dramm had his eye on her since she walked in.

"How are you enjoying that Burgundy?" Dramm asked her.

"It's excellent, thank you. From your private cellar?" she asked.

"Yes, it is. I'm glad you like it. I love Burgundy, but I prefer the color of a Bordeaux better. It's a deeper red that appeals to my senses?" Dramm gave her a suggestive smile.

"Closer to the color of blood?" she asked.

"Well, I wasn't going to bring it up but, now that you have…"

"Now that I have," she interrupted, "you want to discuss it further, correct?"

"You could say that."

"Why do you have a problem with improving the safety of our blood supply?"

"I don't. I have a problem with restricting access to our blood supply."

"What's the difference where my bill is concerned?"

"I just would like some of the rules, as far as end-users are concerned, be less restrictive. If you could adjust the bill for those specifics, I would agree on it. What's wrong with a little compromise?"

"The problem with compromising with others happens when you compromise integrity. I would be willing to work with you on it as long as the objective of the bill remains intact."

"Well, perhaps you could do that if you would walk a mile in my shoes, so to speak."

"And you think that would make me see my bill more objectively?"

Dramm looked around and noticed they were alone in his kitchen. "No, but perhaps you would see it in a different light."

"So how would you propose I see the bill from your point of view?" she asked.

"Let's see, Little Red Riding Hood. Perhaps you've noticed I am Count Dracula."

"Should I fear you?"

"Not at all. I'm not the Big Bad Wolf. But…" Dramm drew his cape over his face and spoke through it as he approached her. "I 'vant to bite your neck."

He wrapped the cape around her in a playful manner, to shield his next action from any onlookers. Dramm sank his teeth into her bare neck.

"Ah…" Dramm clutched his hand to his throat.

He stumbled back and muttered, "Van Helsing."

He collapsed.

****

The press gathered in the Senate Office Building. They took their places in front of the podium. All the networks were there to cover the hastily called press conference. Senator Sheila Osborne stood at the podium and addressed the crowd.

"I called this press conference to announce the Blood Supply Safety Act has been renamed in honor of my esteemed colleague, Senator Dramm. It's now simply the Dramm Act. As you know, he passed away rather unexpectedly. The bill has been passed in both the Senate and the House. We now wait on the President's signature."

"Can you tell us the cause of death of Senator Dramm?" asked a woman reporter.

"Yes, the Senator was suffering from a rare blood disorder. Apparently, it caused a blood clot, which led to a brain hemorrhage."

"Is that why you called this press conference at this late hour?" asked a second woman reporter.

"Yes," added a man reporter, "calling a press conference at this hour is unlike you."

"Yes, it is. Another thing out of character for me is my announcement that I am throwing my hat in the ring for President of the United States."

"That really is out of character for you," said the male reporter.

"Why the sudden change?" asked the first woman reporter.

"Let's just say I have new blood. That's all the questions for now. I have an important meeting to attend. Thank you all for coming."

Osborne walked past the cameras and made her way through the crowd.

****

Osborne entered the hideaway conference room in the Senate Office Building and made her way to the front of the room. She addressed the senators before her, Mikelson, Ryan, and Caparzo.

"Why the low turnout?" she asked. "I thought there would be more of you here."

"You should know," replied Mikelson, "It's a long weekend. Most of Congress has gone home."

"Very well," said Osborn, "This won't take long. I intend to meet the rest of our community as soon as we can reconvene. So, I will tell you what I intend to tell them. Make no mistake, I was an outsider drafted into this position. Furthermore, I expect full cooperation from all of you in my new community."

Senator Caparzo asked, "Do you have any specific plans?"

"Yes, I do. How many more will we need to add to our community to prevent Congress from overriding my vetoes?"

The End

Night Gallery

Hatteras Island Mystery

Review by the late Tom Johnson

- ➤ Title: Hatteras Island Mystery
- ➤ Author: Anne Greene
- ➤ Genre: Romantic Mystery
- ➤ Publisher: Independently Published
- ➤ ISBN: 1690762157
- ➤ Cost: Price $6.74; 130 Pages
- ➤ Available at: Amazon
- ➤ Rating: 5 Stars

Misty Gordon, the local wedding photographer, notices a handsome man unattended at the latest wedding party. The next day she is walking the beach and finds this gentleman floating in the water. Fearing he is dead, Misty pulls him from the water. Discovering he is still alive, she begins asking his names, but he appears to have lost his memory. It looks like someone has tried to kill him, and the police are interested in him and the incident. He escapes from their custody, and Misty helps him recover his identity, falling in love with him in the process.

The author sent me a copy of the book for an honest review. Although the man's name is Quin, a curious note, the pulp character The Black Bat's real name is Tony Quinn. However, Quin also goes by Captain Hazard, another pulp hero. I was further amazed when his million-dollar boat is named *The Doctor Is In*. I remember an article written on Doc Savage titled *The Doctor Is In*. Curious, there are so many tags to pulp characters. Although the mystery was small, the characters were topnotch, and the story was lots of fun. Highly recommended.

Tom Johnson, Author of *The Black Bat Companion*

Murder in One Take

Review by the late Tom Johnson

- ➤ Title: Murder in One Take
- ➤ Authors: April Kelly & Marsha Lyons
- ➤ Genre: Police Procedural
- ➤ Publisher: Flight Risk Books
- ➤ ISBN: 978-0615645339
- ➤ Price: $12.95; 324 Pages
- ➤ Available at: Amazon, Book Depository, and Google Books
- ➤ Rating: 5 Stars

"You'll not want to put this book down."

Detective Blake Ervansky has just met his new partner, Sergeant Maureen O'Brien, and their first assignment together is to arrest a felon. But things quickly go haywire. Before they can reach the felon, a woman shoots and kills a man right in front of them. The victim is a popular actor, and the shooter, also an actress, was his lover. It looks like an open and shut case from the very beginning, and the reader knows who the killer is. Making the arrest, the woman tells them she thought the man was a stalker, mistaking her ex-lover for the stalker. All the clues point in that direction, but Sergeant O'Brien tells her partner the woman is lying. They can't prove it, and the Grand Jury refuses to indict her. The father of the murder victim asks the governor to have Ervansky and O'Brien put on leave from the Beverly Hills Police Department, and into his employ to find the proof of guilt on the shooter.

Although Detective Ervansky and Sergeant O'Brien are the main characters, there are many interesting side characters, well-drawn and fleshed out. There is a lot of good police work, some good guesses on the part of the investigators, and a bit of humor to keep the story from bogging down in too much dark seriousness that clutters so many mystery novels today. The writing is intelligent and excellently paced, the dialogue believable – and humorous. The copy I read was well edited. There was one big problem, however; the novel had no chapters! I had to read the book in one sitting because I could never find a breaking point! Just kidding. This book was a fun read, and I highly recommend it to all mystery lovers. You really may not want to put it down.

Tom Johnson, Publisher of *Detective Mystery Stories*

Cotton FBI Collection # 1

Review by the late Tom Johnson

- ➤ Title: Cotton FBI Collection #1 (FBI Drama, episodes 1 thru 4)
- ➤ Author: Various Authors
- ➤ Genre: FBI Drama, Episodes one through four
- ➤ Publisher: Bastei Entertainment
- ➤ ASIN: B00RTQYBTC
- ➤ Price: $3.99; 337 Pages
- ➤ Available at: Amazon, Barnes & Noble, and Walmart
- ➤ Rating: 5 Stars

"Fast Action, Well Written, With Interesting Characters."

This collection contains four short novels: "The Beginning" by Mario Giordana, "Countdown" by Peter Menninggen, "Hidden Shadows" by Jan Gardemann, and "Witness Protection" by Alexander Lohmann.

"The Beginning" begins when Patrolman Jeremiah Cotton and his partner stop in a seedy part of the city. His partner leaves the car to check on Asian prostitutes that are paying him for protection, something that angers Cotton, but he can't do anything about the situation. More than one cop in the city is crooked. While his partner is away, a Chinese woman passes the patrol car, and he notices a weapon tucked under her blouse in back. Suspicious, he follows her into a building, and hearing the sound of a body crashing to the floor, he enters a room to investigate. As he sees the young woman on the floor in a pool of blood, he senses movement behind him, then the blur of a hand, and he's knocked to the floor. The assailant escapes before he can get up. After calling for assistance, he's arrested when patrols arrive on the scene. Taken to the police station, Cotton is interrogated by the FBI.

The FBI has been investigating a serial killer of Asian prostitutes in several States bordering New York, and the woman Cotton had followed into the building was an FBI Special Agent on the case. When he continues to stick his nose into the investigation, he discovers the unit she was assigned to was the G-Team, a special FBI unit. As Cotton comes up with more clues, the Team eventually allows him in, and the story follows their investigation into an even deeper motive than the murder of prostitutes.

"Countdown" begins when terrorists somehow take control of a passenger plane coming into New York. With a computer, they have taken control away from the pilot and using the plane as a weapon to blackmail America into releasing an Arab prisoner. The plane has six hours of fuel on board, so the case must be solved within that short time. Forced to comply, Cotton and his senior partner, Decker, are sent to the prison to pick the prisoner up in exchange. As they are loading him into the van, a silenced shot fired from the prison, killing the Arab instantly, then the assassin escapes.

As each of their investigations ends in failures, the president closes G-Team after five hours and assigns the job to Homeland Security. They solve the problem in the next hour, destroying the terrorist office and getting the plane down, though the terrorists escaped. Something isn't right about the whole situation, but Cotton can't figure what. Returning to his apartment after being fired, he finds a young girl sitting on the steps, abused and crying. Learning that her father is beating her and his wife, he intervenes, and while helping the girl, something she does snaps his mind toward a clue to the whole case. But will he have time to save the G Team and bring the culprits to justice?

"Hidden Shadows" begins when Cotton and his senior partner, Decker, are called to investigate the death of Dominick Tarbell, the son of Claudia Tarbell, the Secretary of Commerce. He fell from the Brooklyn Bridge, and a bomb followed him down to explode on a boat below.

The case involves illegal drug smuggling to Canada, as well as a terrorist plot against buildings in New York.

"Witness Protection" begins when a woman is found drowned in the New York Harbor with a false ID. The boss of G-Team puts Decker and Cotton on the case, but Cotton doesn't understand why a mere drowning brings in their FBI team. They soon learn that somebody is offering a *witness protection* scheme to people who want to disappear with a lot of money, and this interests the chief of G-Team.

Cotton discovers that there have been other strange deaths of unknown people with false IDs, and other people that have come up missing. It may all add up to the same case. Is the head of the racket working two angles on the disappearances?

These four short novels, each by different authors, set the stage for the new series. The stories are fast, well written, with good plots and lots of pulpy action. Highly recommended.

Tom Johnson, Publisher of *Detective Mystery Stories*

A Blonde for Murder

Review by the late Tom Johnson

- ➤ Title: A Blonde for Murder
- ➤ Author: Walter B. Gibson
- ➤ Genre: Mystery
- ➤ Publisher: Mystery House (www.FictionHousePress.com)
- ➤ ISBN: 978-1505428568
- ➤ Price: $11.67; 230 Pages
- ➤ Available at: Amazon, Barnes & Noble, and Lulu Books
- ➤ Rating: 5 Stars

"A Master Magician Unravels A Murder Mystery."

John Arden, better known as the Great Ardini, is performing for a theater crowd when a young girl being chased by the police rushes on stage, then disappears in one of his famous magic acts. Now the police think Ardini is a suspect in league with the girl in the murder of a private detective working for an insurance company.

It's up to the Great Ardini to find the girl, uncover the plot, and reveal the true murderer. He's up again a spiritualist, another amateur magician, and gangsters, one of which may be the real killer. Ardini brings the case to an explosive end with a séance.

This novel was originally published by Vital Publications in 1948 but holds up well almost 70 years later. The author was a magician, and created several magician detectives, including Norgil the Magician, though this was the first Ardini story I had read. He is better known as the creator and author of *The Shadow*. Highly recommended.

Tom Johnson, Publisher of *Detective Mystery Stories*

Minister's Shoes

Review by the late Tom Johnson

- ➢ Title: Minister's Shoes (A Reverend Castle Mystery)
- ➢ Author: Celine Rose Mariotti
- ➢ Genre: Christian Mystery
- ➢ Publisher: Write Word Inc. www.writewordinc.com
- ➢ ISBN: 9781613862445
- ➢ Price: $18.95; 170 Pages
- ➢ Available at: Amazon and Thrift Books
- ➢ Rating: 4 Stars

"A Good Read."

Reverend Clayton Castle is the pastor of a church in Corning, Alabama, and often gets involved in detective cases. When one of his members asks to see him, he learns that her womanizing husband has disappeared, and she wants Pastor Castle to find him and bring him home. Finding the husband is the easy part, but he turns up in jail for murder, and it appears to involve a casino under construction. Now the reverend has to prove he's not only innocent but bring him back to his wife and away from his illicit affairs.

Remember those scholastic books we read when we were 10 to 12 years old. These were intelligent authors writing for children on the children's level of education. "Minister's Shoes" would have been a perfect fit, even if it does have adult themes. This was a good concept, and I want to encourage the author to continue the series. However, there are several problems with the writing that the author needs to work on. The dialogue was wooden and didn't seem real. The bad guys didn't sound bad, though we have a murderer, an adulterer, gamblers, and gangsters. But everyone acted like good church-going Southern Baptists, praying at every opportunity. God appears in the flesh and talks to the preacher, telling him who to talk to, and what questions to ask, etc. At one point, the preacher is captured by gangsters and even rescued by God. This may not be for everyone, but it's nice to see Christian books published, and I can highly recommend this for children and Christian readers.

Tom Johnson, Publisher of *Detective Mystery Stories*

Murder: Take Two

Review by the late Tom Johnson

- ➤ Title: Murder: Take Two
- ➤ Authors: April Kelly & Marsha Lyons
- ➤ Genre: Murder Mystery
- ➤ Publisher: Flight Risk Books
- ➤ ISBN: 978-0615645348
- ➤ Price: $14.95; 396 Pages
- ➤ Available at: Amazon, Barnes & Noble, and Thrift Books
- ➤ Rating: 5 Stars

"Fast-Paced, Easy Reading, With Fascinating Characters."

Ex-police detectives Blake Ervansky & Maureen O'Brien are now working as private investigators at their E&O Investigations in Hollywood when Maureen suddenly disappears. Her father tells Blake not to worry, she will be back, but can't tell him where she is. Upon her return, Blake learns that his partner was involved as an assassin with the CIA before coming to work in the BHPD, and this worries him. What is he doing working with a trained government assassin? But her background just might come in handy with their current assignment. E&O is hired by a rich entertainer from Nevada to find her missing husband, who she suspects has been murdered by his magician partner.

Setting up camp in Madison, Nevada, where the magician has his compound with the caged tigers from his act, the investigators quickly learn that the killer has the sheriff and town in his pocket. If they are going to prove their client's husband was murdered, they will have to come up with a little magic of their own.

This is the second novel in the Ervansky & O'Brien series and proves that the authors weren't one-hit wonders. This second novel, filled with intrigue and humor, takes up where the first novel left off. The prose is fast-paced, easy reading with imaginative characters, and a great plot. With no chapter breaks, it's a reading marathon, as the reader hates to put the book down until the final page – and it's almost 400 pages in length! The writing is humorous, while the dialogue is realistic, though the reader must keep in mind that this is Hollywood, where things might not be like they are elsewhere. I got a real kick out of the scene where Maureen's father breaks out in song with a waitress, like some Hollywood musical. Highly recommended for mystery fans, and any lover of entertainment.

Tom Johnson, Publisher of *Detective Mystery Stories*

Bloody January

Review by the late Tom Johnson

- ➤ Title: Bloody January
- ➤ Author: Alan Parks
- ➤ Genre: Crime
- ➤ Publisher: Europa Editions (World Noir Imprint)
- ➤ ISBN: 978-1609454487
- ➤ Price: $17.00 (paperback); $8.69 (Kindle); 331 Pages
- ➤ Available at: Amazon, Barnes & Noble, and Canongate Books
- ➤ Rating: 3 Stars

I was given a copy of the book from the publisher for an honest review. Detective Harry McCoy doesn't always play by the rules, but he's a tough cop, and won't stop his investigation once on the scent. Receiving a tip about an upcoming murder, he dives in only to be met with obstacles from the rich and influential, as well as his own superiors in the "shop."

This is Glasgow in 1973, and the author paints a picture of its citizens and seedy byways in a panorama of visual scenes and characters in the turmoil of drugs, sex, incest, and murder, where it's difficult to distinguish the upper class from the sewer rats.

This was a good mystery, with good characters, but I can't help thinking it could have been handled with more finesse. We have bright, intelligent, educated characters that have trouble speaking words longer than four letters, and the profanity was above board, in my opinion. The story could have used a little less profanity and a bit more intelligent thought, perhaps.

Tom Johnson, Author of *The Man in the Black Fedora*

Reg 25
by
Rod Marsden

Reg 25, who was the twenty-fifth to register under the name Reg in his district, was sneered at by a twenty-something woman with blue hair as he started his walk to work. He didn't say anything or do anything. He suspected she blamed him for the mess the country was in, but he was only one man. What could he have done about the Globalist takeover?

Young people were now in full support of Globalisation. If not, there were rehabilitation centres. He had spent some time in one. He emerged just as distraught about where he was living and why, so it didn't have the desired effect. The people there yelled at him and called him a grub because he grew up before Globalisation took hold and so couldn't possibly understand the glory of it. In that they were right.

Reg 25 went past the latest demonstration. He didn't bother to see what it was about because it didn't matter. He thought it might have something to do with whether Wollongong should be importing shoes from parts of Nationalist China rather than from good old Globalist China. Only Globalist demonstrations were permitted. Anything else was brutally suppressed. Hence there had to be student support for Globalist Chinese shoes. Shoes from either part of China fell apart after about six months of wear, so for him, it wasn't a big deal.

A man in a black uniform came up to him. Was he army or militia? Both wore black, but the badges on their caps were different. Both carried truncheons and were happy to use them on anyone they felt wasn't feeling especially Globalist that day. Citizens such as Reg 25 wore grey in solidarity – or else! The last person of his vintage who wore anything colourful in either Melbourne or Sydney got stomped on first by good Globalist citizens, then beaten up by militia and thrown in jail. He died in lockup. Reg 25 hummed a popular Globalist solidarity tune as he made his way past the man in black uniform. The man in black uniform nodded his approval.

Reg 25 was hungry, so he stopped at an eatery. Today, they were serving bits of dried fish in boiled rice. There was something small and orange in his bowl. It might have been part of a carrot. This made him feel hopeful. He remembered he liked carrots but hadn't seen a whole carrot in years.

Wollongong, where Reg 25 lived and worked, wasn't as bad as Melbourne or Sydney just as those cities were not as bad as London and New York, where Globalism first took hold. Nearby to New York, Philadelphia was still fiercely Nationalistic and would be so for the foreseeable future. Reg 25 suspected the food was better there than in London, New York, Sydney, Melbourne, and Wollongong. Greek and Italian restaurants were still in operation, and fresh greens were coming into Philadelphia daily from Michigan. At least that's what some woman his vintage had told him. He had no way of confirming whether it was true or not.

In the Wollongong newspaper he bought off the waiter, he read an article about Italy. The tragedy of the day was the Italian Nationalists taking back Rome from the Globalists. They were also, together with the Greeks, pushing Globalist forces back to Tunisia. It seemed to Reg 25 the Italians and the Greeks would continue to fight to remain Italians and Greeks for a long time to come.

Elsewhere in Europe, the people of Poland and Hungary had joined forces against German and French Globalists. An underground French movement started by Le Penn decades ago was helping to supply the Poles with much needed ammunition, including rockets and rocket launchers, to fight against French and German tanks.

Then there was news from Russia. A Tsar and Tsarina had been appointed to rule over the people and lead the new revolution against Globalism. They were from the same province Stalin had come from and were all about fear, intimidation, and reward where that would be useful to them. This was not how many Russians wanted to be ruled, but they had looked at what Globalism had done to London and New York and felt that the return of the Tsar and Tsarina suited them marginally better. At least it was traditional.

In New York, an Asian journalist, who had gone insane with hatred for white people, had committed suicide soon after she had brought Globalism to her city. Maybe white people weren't so bad after all. Perhaps multicultural New York had been okay being multicultural.

While he ate his meal, there was a happy community's reality show on the flat-screen positioned above the waiter. It came with a simple but catchy tune of togetherness at the start. Its mental syrup didn't flow too far into Reg 25's brain. It got banked up by his memories of a far better time when crazy do-gooders were a joke, and people were allowed to laugh at themselves and fly the Australian flag. Now that could only be done in Hobart, Tasmania, which was a Nationalist holdout.

Reg 25 washed down his fish and rice with weak tea. Coffee was too expensive and could only be bought by section leaders and men and women in black uniforms because they could afford it. He was too old and thought not indoctrinated well enough to ever be a section leader.

The greasy-haired waiter that had provided him with breakfast and the newspaper had been suspicious of him.

"Aren't they rounding up your sort?" he asked.

"My sort?" enquired Reg 25 defensively.

"*The Paul Hogan Show, Kingswood Country, Acropolis Now, Mary Poppins,*" counted off the waiter. "Someone as old as you grew up with that stuff, didn't you?"

"I am a loyal Globalist!" cried Reg 25.

"Sure, you are!" cried back the waiter sarcastically. "Sure, you are!"

Reg 25 left the eatery feeling low but pepped himself up by thinking of those Italian Nationalists in Rome. He was a mild fellow who tried to avoid politics but couldn't help but find pleasure where and when Nationalists did well.

He was expected to work in a glue factory until he was eighty, and he hadn't complained about that the way some poor souls had. He had nothing to say when the internet was dismantled in the name of Globalist unity. He hadn't cheered like some fools did when Nationalists blew up the United Nations building in New York some years ago. It didn't do any good, though, since the Globalists just built a new one to take its place.

The glue factory helped make the sky permanently grey. Everyone knew it, but no one was allowed to say anything. The fact that everyone lived in high-rises and houses didn't exist anymore because the people who had owned them were selfish also contributed to the muck. Pile more and more people into a smaller and smaller space, and something has got to give.

Also, the water along the beaches was kind of grey, and the sand no longer as yellow as it had once been. In the summer, you had to listen to reports to know when it was safe to swim.

Mind you, swimming had changed. The costumes worn were much what you would find expressed in a 1901 sports catalogue. Wear anything that might be considered provocative or Nationalistic and expect to get beaten to death then taken out to sea for the sharks to feast on. The last woman to wear a bikini was stoned to death by an angry mob then boated to where sharks could eat her corpse.

Reg 25 hadn't gone swimming in years. He remembered too well the freedom that had existed on those beaches before the Globalists took over. He was too aware of what had progressively been taken away.

Representatives from the United Nations walked briskly past Reg 25 as he further made his way to where he had to sit for five hours, putting lids on cans. These representatives were permitted to wear light sky blue with a white symbol of the world on the right chest side of their uniform. They were the only ones not in either black or grey. Reg 25 wondered where there might still be skies that were sometimes blue. He suspected it would have to be in Nationalist-held territory.

Reg 25 showed his pass to get past the official factory gatekeeper who wanted to catch him just once without his pass so she could fine him. The gatekeeper, as per usual, looked at him with contempt, at the pass, nodded, and let him in. His fellow workers were old like him. Some had collapsed and passed away on their shift and been taken away when their shift ended. This was what he was expected to do – die!

After five hours of mind-numbing activity listening to cheery nonsense, he went to the cafeteria for lunch. He had mashed potatoes and beans washed down with a weak orange drink. He counted the beans. There were four. Yesterday there were only three.

On the cafeteria screen was a program on how beneficial to all Globalism has been and how everyone should join in the battle against those horrid, selfish Nationalists with their old-fashioned ways of life. Cricket? Not for me! Baseball? Decadent! Join in for a nice sing-along as our forces march to victory! Jogging and calisthenics if you want to be part of the human race and beat those who refuse to see the world the way we do! Basketball for everyone! There's a court near you! Don't be shy! Be part of a winning team! Go jog with your neighbours! They'll love you for it.

There were recent victories shown. Resistance in the state of Florida in the USA had broken down. Nationalist cells could not remain hidden in those swamps forever. Tasmanian ships had been fired upon and sunk.

What weren't shown were the defeats which were barely touched upon in the local newspaper that morning. Sure, the Florida cells of the Nationalists were finished, but the Mississippi Nationalists were doing just fine. Sure, some Tasmanian ships were sunk, but more Globalist vessels had gone under in that skirmish.

The Western world is being taken over, and there is nothing I can do about it, thought Reg 25. *Thank God there is still resistance somewhere. I bet the people living in Tasmania still eat well. Here food production is way down and population continually on the rise. Why are we being punished like this? Why were we so naive? Open borders all the way! No one wins, we all lose and yet these black-uniformed fools want to celebrate!*

Grudgingly, Reg 25 went back to putting lids on cans. He had five more hours of it plus the stupid music. This was followed by that walk home to the tiny box he had in an enormous high-rise. There he was expected to watch two hours of mind-killing reality television before retiring. If he did not, then neighbours listening in would report him as a Nationalist subversive.

He had a boiled egg and a meatball in his fridge to eat for supper. He also had watered down lemon juice. It was something to anticipate. He suspected there might actually be meat this time in the meatball.

On his walk home, a dozen young men and women confronted him, blocking his way.

"Hey! Old man!" cried out the leader, a shaven-headed woman in her early twenties and fake black leather. "You watched *Skippy* when you were a boy? You watched *Hogan's Heroes* or *McHale's Navy*? You read *A Fortunate Life* or *I Can Jump Puddles*?"

"I suppose I might have," Reg 25 replied.

"I know!" cried a young man of African appearance who looked to be sporting real leather dyed black. "What about *Robin Hood*?"

"Ha! Sold to you for a pretty penny way back near the beginning of the 21st century." Reg 25 laughed bitterly at the youth of African appearance.

"What's that?" asked the shaven-headed leader. "Elaborate, you old sponge!"

"Ah! Let's see if I can remember," said Reg 25. "Legend once had it that Robin Hood formed a band of Saxons to defend England from tyranny while King Richard was away. Norman lords were brutally overtaxing the Saxons, and there was much suffering. Robin Hood and his men sought to put a stop to that."

"What's a Saxon?" asked a pink-haired young woman.

"What a Norman?" the guy in real leather asked.

"Exactly!" cried Reg 25. "All gone! All forgotten!"

"Speak plainly!" warned the leader. "Sounds like you need rehabilitation!"

"The British Broadcasting Corporation took an English legend and set about pulling it apart, making it no longer English," said Reg 25. "Friar Tuck could no longer be early English, a Saxon. He had to be something else, and he could no longer be a friar. For over four hundred years, in legend, that's what he was, but that was all thrown out for early 21st century television viewing."

"Why?" the guy in real leather asked.

"For you," said Reg 25, almost laughing bitterly at the irony of the question, "to make you comfortable!"

"Really?" the guy in authentic leather asked. He was astonished. "I was made comfortable?"

"Oh, yes," said Reg 25. "But it was more than just your comfort. If you want to destroy a people, you first take away their legends and give them to someone else. The British Broadcasting Corporation, back when I was younger, was all about doing just that. There was a movie out back then also that had John Little, also known as Little John, as something other than a Saxon forester gone outlaw. He was a historical character, but that didn't save him. No, indeed, it did not save him at all."

"Why are you telling us all this?" asked the leader. "You know we will report you for rehabilitation."

"Oh, I'm just remembering," said Reg 25 timidly. "The British Broadcasting Corporation also put out a television show called *Troy*. Instead of having Achilles as a blond-haired Greek that satisfied legend, he had to be something else. I am not sure why, but they had to attack the Greeks this way. It had something to do with the political correctness of the time."

"The Greeks are our enemies," said the leader.

"Oh, yes!" agreed Reg 25. "The present-day Greeks and the Italians too are Nationalists. Is Ned Kelly still an Irish Australian? I thought I'd ask."

"Ned who?" said the leader. "Is this Ned Kelly a friend of yours?"

"Never mind," Reg 25 mused. "All gone! All forgotten! The Australian Broadcasting Corporation, in the end, was also thorough, it would seem, in dismantling history."

"Does anyone have any further questions for this filth?" asked the leader.

"Oh! I know!" put in a short, black-haired fellow in his late teens also in fake leather. "You used to go to the Returned Serviceman's League for your dinner on Saturdays before they were all closed down! Is this true?"

"Ha! I bet you this creep was all for ANZAC Day," said the teenage girl with pink hair. "He might even be an ANZAC. Are you an ANZAC, Granddad? Did you kill any third-world babies, Granddad? You do that? Did you?"

"No," replied Reg 25. "I never did that. I killed no one. I wanted to kill no one. I was never in uniform. Now please let me go!"

"But you did take a holiday on ANZAC Day when it was a holiday, is that right?" prompted the black-haired fellow with fake leather.

"Everyone did," Reg 25 told him.

"You didn't think that was wrong at the time?" asked the shaven-headed woman who was the leader.

"No, I didn't," Reg 25 replied. "No one said it was wrong at the time except a few people on television. I think that was said on the Australian Broadcasting Corporation station."

"But you say it was wrong now because you are a supporter of Globalisation, is that right?" asked the pink-haired girl.

"I suppose I do," said Reg 25. "I support Globalisation."

"Liar!" screamed the teenage girl with the pink hair.

"Liar!" cried the shaven-headed woman who then hit Reg 25 with her fist. "We'll rehabilitate this bastard now our way!"

They beat him and he collapsed under the beating. Then they went away, and he had to make it to his feet somehow. His box wasn't far away, but it was up three flights of steps and the elevator was out. It was a struggle, but he made it to his door. He could barely scrape it open with his keys.

He fell onto his lounge chair, ignoring the discomfort of the fact it was falling into ruin. He switched on the television screen and drifted off to sleep. His upper lip was swollen, so he wasn't very hungry. The egg and meatball could wait. Maybe he'd have his lemon juice when he felt like getting to it. He knew one of his eyes was swelling up and tearing.

What did those young people want, a confession? He had nothing to confess. He hadn't created the world they were living in now. The politicians did that. Two major parties and they had the same goal. The members of those parties wanted to make money for themselves and to hell with the people they were supposed to be serving. That was Australia back in the early 21st century.

Other countries had similar problems with their politicians. They bowed to the United Nations, and the United Nations bowed to those who ruled over the oil-rich lands as well as to other parts of the planet that despised the West. Thus, the downfall of the West these young people were now living through was assured.

Maybe it all did go wrong with Vietnam way back in the 20th century. Some of Reg 25's contemporaries thought so. Maybe 9/11 was the great catalyst in the early 21st century. None of that mattered anymore except to historians.

Reg 25 reasoned that the wars between Nationalists and Globalists would eventually turn into religious strife. He could see, for example, Christian versus Muslim. He thought Sikhs and Buddhists would stay out of it as much as possible but would get dragged in on one side or the other the same as atheists and agnostics. In holy wars no one could be innocent or safe. You picked a side, or you died. It was as simple as that. You might die anyway. All this Reg 25 could see as he dreamed of a dark and evil future. It was a dream that would last him the rest of his life.

The Old One on his cloud in another dimension had been observing Reg 25. He was so typical of the men of his time and place. In his last dying moments, on that rubbishy old lounge chair, however, Reg 25 had insights that were fresh as well as surprisingly accurate.

Holy wars were coming. They were the only events to justify the hardships already felt by too many people living in too many countries in the West. It would be reminiscent of ancient madness but nothing to do with the Old One who would enjoy such goings-on immensely through the globe that showed him Earth. He had no need to manipulate these happenings. Humanity was now on the right road to its own destruction and the return of his kind to the planet.

It was nine the following morning after Reg 25 was reported late for work that the landlord let officers of the law into Reg 25's box. There they found him still watching television.

They shook him, but he failed to respond. They then turned off the set and summoned a doctor. After his death was confirmed, a sanitation vehicle came to collect Reg 25 and his meagre possessions.

All were dumped, including Reg 25, into a landfill to be later covered up. Within a day, a new tenant moved into where Reg 25 used to live, and life of a sort continued for some though not for others.

The End

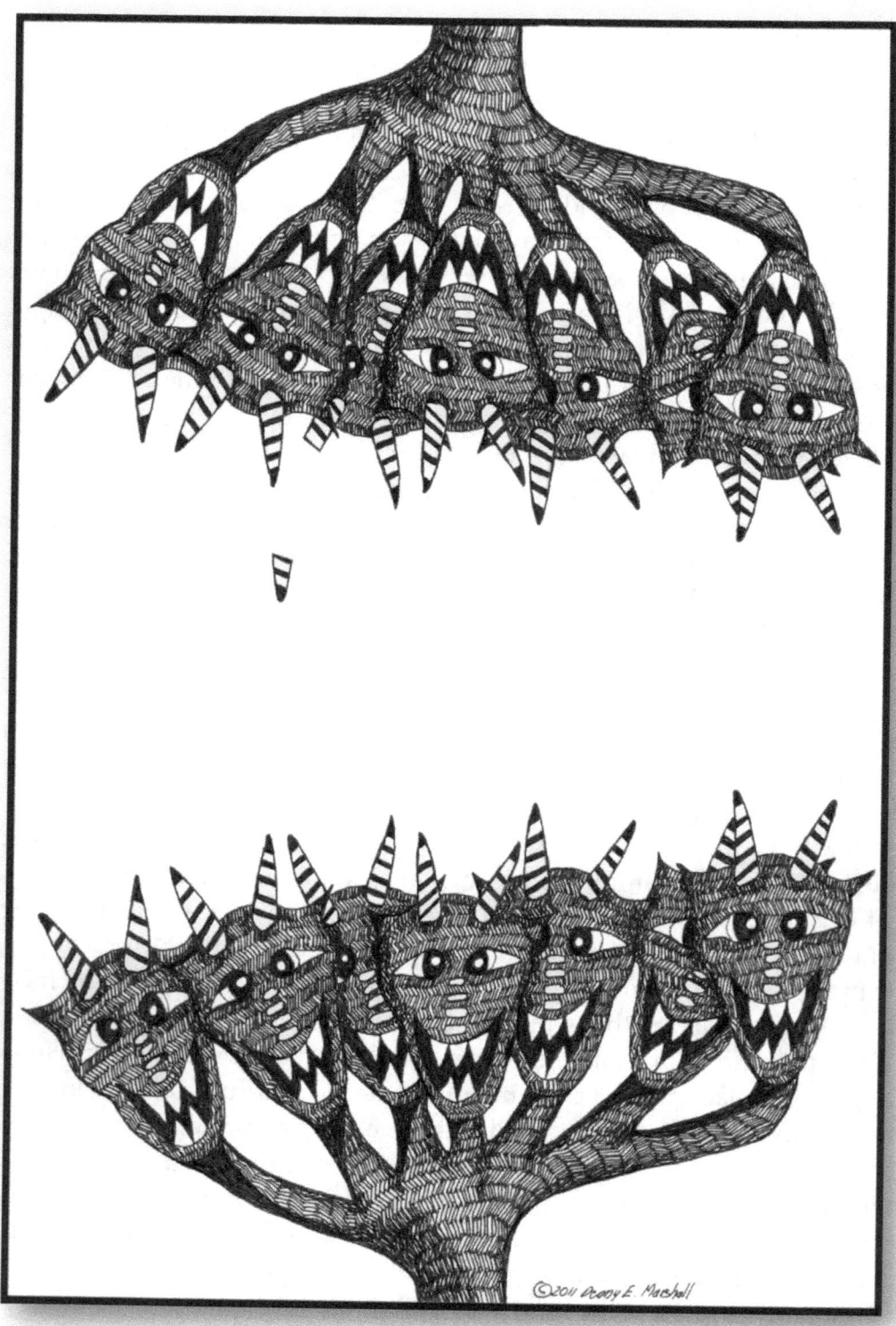

Zuguh: Abomination from Hell
by
Rajeev Bhargava

Padre Wolfe, a frail high priest in his mid-nineties, was on the verge of closing his church door when a young lady came running towards him. Alarmed, he placed his frail hands over his face. She fell at his feet and held his legs, breaking down in a fit of tears. He removed his hands and looked down at her.

"My child, what is the matter? Please get up." He helped her to her feet. "Why are you in tears? Did someone hurt you?"

"Padre Wolfe, only you can help me." She fought back tears as she spoke. "I was expecting my baby, but it was stillborn. Now, my heart is broken. It's the third time and quite frankly…" She burst in tears again.

"How tragic. I wish I could bring your baby back to life, but that power is in God's hands."

"I wish I was dead. My life has no value. I'm going to commit suicide."

"No! Do not ever let this thought enter your mind again. It is the greatest and most unforgivable sin. Promise me!" Padre Wolfe gave her a tight hug.

"I don't know what to do." She cried and cried until Padre Wolfe's face lit up.

"I think I have the answer to your pain. But you will need to pass a test."

"Anything. Just name it."

"Follow me." He hesitated. "Wait, what's your name?"

"Delilah Forester."

Holding her right arm, Padre Wolfe led her through the church and out the back exit. There was a long narrow trail. It was pitch-black outside. Just then, he stopped and pointed at a misshapen fleshy lump lying by the gutter. It was making muffled crying sounds, almost in whimpers.

Padre Wolfe approached it, then knelt. He lifted and cradled it in his arms, humming a lullaby.

"What is it, Padre?" asked Delilah, bewildered.

"I've named it Zuguh. Behold, here is a child. Your child."

"But what was it doing lying here? Is it even human?"

"It's a very long tale to tell. One night, as I had finished my sermon, I heard these strange whimpers as you hear now. After everyone had left, I found it. I dared not mention it to anyone, in case they would try to harm it. I don't even know if its mother may turn up. If she does, I will inform her that her baby is being cared for by you. This is *your* test, Delilah. God be with you. Go now, and remember to hide it away and nurture it with love."

"Oh, thank you, Padre!" And with those words, Delilah cradled the baby in her arms and rushed back home.

****

"Coochy-coo. Coochy-coo! Now, I had better place you somewhere safe, Zuguh dear, before Terry comes home from work."

Delilah Forester carried the baby into the kitchen and perched it on a chair. She then browsed through the cupboards until she found a box of rusks. She handed one to the baby, just as the front door opened.

"Wait here, dear, I'll be back shortly." As she turned away, the baby's eyes rolled inside out, and worms slid from its sockets.

"Hello, Delilah." Her husband Terry wrapped his arms around her and gave her a passionate kiss.

"How was work today?" asked Delilah. "Is Mr. Forbes still harassing you?"

"No. If he was, then I wouldn't feel like dancing." Once again, he reached out to Delilah and waltzed around the hallway with her. She suspected some good news.

"Oh, I think I understand. You got promoted, right?"

He released her and tutted. "How did you guess?"

"Body language." Delilah shrugged. Just then, there was a loud thud accompanied by crunching sounds. Both turned and looked at the kitchen door.

"What was that noise?" Terry asked.

"Wait here, I'll find out." Delilah rushed inside and gasped. There on the kitchen floor, the baby was crawling about, coated in blood. Panicking, she whirled around and banged into Terry, who was standing right behind her, mouth gaping in disbelief and horror.

"What the hell is *that monstrosity*!"

"Oh, Terry! I'm so sorry. I meant to surprise you. I would like to introduce you to Baby Zuguh."

"Oh, no. Please don't tell me that uncanny creepy-crawly is a baby. Why, it's not even human, is it?" He stepped closer and gazed at it. "Delilah, please be honest with me. Where did you find it? And more importantly, why did you bring it here? It looks so evil. I think it might be a ... a zombie."

"Oh, silly-billy. I found it lying abandoned by some garbage. No one was around, so I brought it home."

"So, you decided to pick it up and bring it home..." Terry frowned.

Upon hearing these words, Zuguh let out a pained cry, then crawled toward Terry's left leg.

"Aww, don't be so heartless, dear. It's only a child."

"I mean, even you're referring to the gender of the baby as 'it.' I meant to say..."

Just then, Zuguh bit into his leg and tore out a piece of flesh, then crawled back under the table and savoured it. Terry fell to the floor, screaming and grabbing his leg.

"Delilah, call an ambulance!"

Delilah reached for the phone, then paused. She felt a maternal pull of protection towards the zombie-baby.

"Well, what are you waiting for!?"

"No, there isn't time. I'll go and get my first aid kit."

As she left, Terry stared in horror at Zuguh. He was genuinely petrified.

"I don't know who or what you are, Zuguh, but I can bet my life that you emerged from the gates of Hell. I have no qualms with you. Please leave us both in peace."

Zuguh swallowed the flesh and giggled. Blood mixed with saliva dribbled from his mouth onto his shrunken stark-naked body. Terry could only gaze back in open-mouthed horror and confusion until his head reeled. Darkness followed...

****

"Where am I?" Terry's eyes burst open and he found himself lying on a trolley bed, covered with a white sheet and a name tag attached to his right toe. Pulling the sheet aside, he looked around. He was in a freezing room, surrounded by corpses. Then, to his shock, one of them, a middle-aged lady, came alive. She had no eyeballs, just empty black pits. She made a menacing groaning sound. Cradling her arms, she walked up to his bed.

"Keep away from me. Keep away!" Terry got up and staggered to the nearest door.

"Help! Help!!"

The zombie fell, lifeless again, onto the floor just as the locked door opened. One of the staff walked in, a man in his late thirties. He stared at Terry, wide-eyed.

"How did you come to life? You were dead when we brought you in here."

"Oh, get out of my way!" Terry retorted. He stormed off, still in his hospital clothes.

****

At home, Delilah had a visitor. It was Terry's boss, Stephen Forbes.

"Sorry to bother you, Delilah. Is your husband in?"

"No. He was rushed to Accident and Emergency yesterday, and declared dead upon arrival." She broke into tears.

"Delilah, there's something I need to tell you." Just as he spoke, Zuguh crawled into the hallway from the kitchen, his mouth still dribbling with Terry's blood.

"Oh, my word! What is *that*?"

"Hey, don't talk that way about my Zuguh."

Mr. Forbes knelt down to take a closer look.

"What's wrong with it? Is it a boy or a girl? It looks … demonic."

Zuguh floated into the air until it reached Mr. Forbes' head. It came towards him then ripped away his nose. Mr. Forbes fled the house, bleeding and screaming.

"Zuguh! That was really naughty," Delilah scolded.

Zuguh giggled, chomping and enjoying its feast.

"Hmm, I wonder what he wanted to tell me."

****

Later that night, Terry tiptoed back into the house, wary that Zuguh could be anywhere. He entered the bedroom to find Deborah curled up in bed with Zuguh.

"Delilah!" Terry brushed his right hand over her legs. She awoke.

"You … you're alive!" She shouted.

"Shhh! There's something I need to tell you alone."

She followed him into the hall and looked around, wondering where Mr. Forbes had gone. "Yes, what is it, Terry, dear?"

"I think I met Zuguh's mother at the hospital mortuary, where the corpses are kept."

"And…?"

"She's one of the undead, too. She wants Zuguh back, or else something terrible will happen to you. She warned me."

"Terry, just listen to yourself."

"I know it sounds crazy, but I think Zuguh's real mother is going to take over your body or turn you into one of the undead."

"Or Zuguh himself?" They turned to see Zuguh, who had transformed into a humanoid figure. It had formed lips. Its mouth opened, calling out, "Maa Maa." Its voice had an amphibious croak.

In the next instant, a trail of smoke filled the hallway, and through it emerged the undead woman Terry had seen. She gazed at Zuguh with a pitiful look and reached out to her child. Delilah dashed forwards and lifted Zuguh in her arms.

"Don't you dare touch my Zuguh!"

Zuguh's mother let out a loud hiss and screamed. From her mouth, millions of maggots spewed and showered Delilah. In the background, Terry appeared with a mallet and made a run towards Zuguh's mother. She turned to him, wide-eyed and furious, then gazed at the mallet. It glowed, hotter and hotter, and gelled onto Terry's arm, until he burst into flames. Moments later, his skeleton lay on the floor, amidst a heap of ashes.

"Terry!" cried Delilah.

"Give me back my child, or else you will also die!" Her voice was loud and shrill.

"You don't scare me, you fiend," said Delilah. "If you really loved Zuguh, then why did you abandon her?"

"Because she's not from our Earth, my child. She's from the very gates of Hell itself!" spoke a familiar voice. Delilah swung around to find Padre Wolfe standing behind her. He held a pure silver cross in both hands and aimed it at the monstrous woman.

"Padre Wolfe, oh, I'm so pleased to see you, but how did you get in?" Delilah asked

"Fortunately, your main door was left open."

"Oh, Padre, what should I do?"

He pointed to the trail of fire, then Zuguh's mother. "This monstrosity walks on flames. These flames begin from the gates of Hell. And now I have to make a painful decision." He gazed at both women and then stroked Zuguh.

"What decision?" Delilah asked, bewildered. "And what about this test you mentioned earlier?"

"Oh, you have passed my test. You have proved that you love Zuguh more than her. She had tossed it down from Hell, so it crashed into the gutter at the back of my church. On a humanitarian basis, I decided to raise it. It was just a tiny ball of flesh, but it made sounds, and it was alive. I was not sure what to make of it. Was it good, was it evil? I had no idea." There was a long, thoughtful pause, then he continued. "I could easily have reported it and had it taken away, but I would never have forgiven myself. You see … it was a question of morals." Tears trickled down Padre Wolf's eyes, and he gazed up. "Lord, if I have committed a sin to protect and raise this fellow mortal, who does not look, act, or behave like us humans, then please forgive me." He took a deep sigh, then composed himself and stared at Zuguh's mother.

"What is your name, oh evil and callous demoness?"

"Bhooparrah," she replied in the same high-pitched, croaky voice.

"Be careful of her, Padre," Delilah cut in. "She's now one of the undead. Terry told me she was actually a dead body in the hospital mortuary."

Padre Wolfe looked at Delilah and Bhooparrah, then said, "Well, if neither of you can decide who the child rightfully belongs to, then I shall." He snapped his fingers and called out at the main door, "You can come on in now, Woolum, and do your dance of death."

They all gazed at the door as a dark burly man of ten feet tall, with red and black symbols painted on his body, emerged. He began an uncanny tribal dance. He sang aloud and stamped his large feet. Each time he did so, Zuguh's mother temporarily began to fade. As he quickened his pace and danced faster and faster, she looked at him helplessly. And then, in a split-second, she leaped forward and grabbed Zuguh, and then, both vanished. Delilah had just managed to blink her eyes and react to what had happened. Woolum stopped his act and stood behind Padre Wolfe.

60

"It is done."

"Thank you, Woolum, you may leave now." Woolum bowed his head and left. Padre' Wolfe' turned to Delilah.

"I'm so sorry about your husband, Terry. May his soul rest in peace."

"And what about my Zuguh?" she asked.

"Take comfort in the fact that you have passed the Lord's test and proven that you look for the good, even in the evilest and callous monstrosities. Now, rest assured, God will have a beautiful reward awaiting you, perhaps in the form of a new life partner and a child of your very own. The Lord works in mysterious ways, Delilah, my child."

"Thanks, Padre Wolfe. I will definitely attend your sermons more regularly. One final question."

"Ask away, my child."

"Who was Woolum?"

"Perhaps an angel come to help us?" He winked and smiled, then added, "Take good care of yourself; only good things come to good people like you. Goodnight, and God bless you."

The End.

Dicing with LIBITINA, Goddess of Funerals and Burials by Rajeev Bhargava

In the dead of night, in the corner of a desolate space, in pindrop silence,
a cloaked figure with a scythe sat crouched, clenching a dice in her hands;
but the "numerals" etched on it were symbols, representing her victim's fate.
The Grim Reaper reached out her bony left hand, then tossed it to the ground
and looked across and gazed at her victim, sneering at his helplessness.
The victim, a young man in his twenties, sat petrified and frozen,
awaiting his fate; the sweat pouring profusely down his forehead.
The dice span magically, in slow motion on the wet ground, turning blood-red,
ultimately revealing his fate; to be punished in a blaze of flames,
but that would only be the finale: after each of his limbs were twisted off
very slowly, ensuring he lives and endures all essence of the pain she inflicted,
because for him, Death was the merciful release of his punishment for
Dicing with LIBITINA, Goddess of funerals and burials...

The Scourge of Zarablaan
by
Lee Clark Zumpe

Below a towering column of burnt-brick which sent shadows streaming over Bel-ah'zund's sandy streets, and beneath the sinuous tendrils of flowering, fragrant herbage in Zur Qumattai's gardens verdurous, was a grievous pact I fool-heartedly embraced. To the black-tongued monarch, whose name had bled from the mouths of one hundred thousand slaves in death, I bartered without consideration my stalwart loyalties for a scant parcel of immortality. I played a pathetic beggar for the seemingly glorious prize he offered; and now, a doleful fool I feel for ingesting wholly that loathsome proposal.

It was but a season ago when I was summoned to stand before his throne; yet it seems as if only a handful of heartbeats have gone by since that day.

His lions golden-clad had scarcely retired their weapons after their return from far-off Suntanakri when once more he called upon his angels of war. Soldiers wearied and worn donned their gleaming helms of bronze and without question or complaint rallied for Zur Qumattai's crusade with their undying fiery zeal.

"To Zarablaan!" cried the Zur.

Aye, to gilded Zarablaan they would march that very day at the charge of the black-tongued monarch. To Zarablaan, that foreboding and cryptic citadel which at the desert's heart sat like a crouching colossus too cumbersome to migrate yet too stubborn to wither and die. To Zarablaan, they would march, swords flashing.

Every man, no matter how old or how youthful, no matter how wise or how addle-headed they might be, knew well the tales that twined like vipers around that distant citadel. The rumpled old war-dogs of Bel-ah'zund in their colorful yarns muttered of wicked Zarablaanian wizards who prattled at leisure with things nidorous and vile, and of the folk there who took great pleasure in devouring their own dead, kith and kin. Such legends were whispered throughout the lands, and it was widely accepted that within that demon-haunted acropolis, sinister and strange hell-born desert-spirits long ago converged and had since lorded it over the sad mortal denizens.

To Zarablaan, Zur Qumattai sent four delbraths of his valiant and never-before thwarted soldiers.

And I, vain soldier risen from the ranks, did Zur Qumattai commission to oversee this ruinous campaign. My ascension lacked both pageantry and pomp, for the silken-robed Zur of Bel-ah'zund beckoned me to his leafy gardens and once there charged me with the office of khmaisi. I would command his four delbraths, each ten thousand warriors strong; and, moreover, a dozen and three supply men would heed my call. For but the glory of the post would I have welcomed the appointment; but a gem seemingly indeclinable Qumattai offered up to me to tighten his invisible grasp upon me.

Locked behind those mountainous walls of Zarablaan, which in the ruthless desert sun shone with copper brilliance, was a mystic object of nebulous origins which the very populace of Zarablaan was committed to defend. More precious than the survival of the city and more valued than the lives of all its citizens was this mysterious treasure which Zur Qumattai imparted to me. Of such consequence was this thing that as sentinels, the web of netherworlds pitchy and arcane had ushered in a host of fetid, darkling rogues. So malign were they that their mere image could cause a pure man's heart to burst—and so it followed thusly that in Zarablaan, not a pure man dwelled.

That which was so hoarded by its keepers and was disclosed to me, was to the Zur revealed in a nightly vision; the Jewel of Kwilaleut it was named. Those oracular and phantasmal sages of Qumattai's dreams urged him to send henceforth forces to seize the Jewel. Those who possess the jewel, claimed he, need not worry over their sources of sustenance, nor fret over the outcome of a battles waged by their armies in distant lands, nor even fear the threat of death. Though its precise properties he deliberately left undefined and its potency he intentionally withheld, I became as obsessed with its liberation from Zarablaan as Qumattai himself. Only now can the spring of my unrelenting longing be recognized; only now can I discern the fountain of dark sorcery which governed me.

And so quickly we put behind us the fertile lands of Bel-ah'zund and made way for the inhospitable and barren lands of the southern marches. The emerald fields and flourishing forests soon gave way to the hostile steppe-country; and in little time, almost all trace of life was gone from the lands over which we advanced.

Across the feverish land of desert waste, we swept, gorged on our patriotism and pride, and thirsting for bloody battle and for conquest over Zarablaan. Over dunes of scorched sand shifted by blistering winds, I led my delbraths four, gloating over the fact that I commanded this noble force.

When finally that ominous citadel peered above the distant horizon, its silvery spires twinkling atop the jade skulls of sacred cupolas, not a single man in forty thousand was found beset by a sliver of fear. And when the silhouetted shapes of defenders were observed weaving eccentricity on the rim of that enormous wall, figures which at a distance might or might not have been men, not one soldier in my command hesitated even fleetingly.

At my command, the forerunners rose high their banner wands which bore the standard of Zur Qumattai. Our colors tossed with the wind as they were unfurled, and the men gave up an ardent, fiery war cry. The defenders replied, and from behind the walls we heard their strange calls-to-arms. Though it must have been horns which they trumpeted to rouse Zarablaan, the sound itself was more akin to the maddened howl of a stalked animal. That hail shall echo in my head forever, I believe.

We lay siege to formidable Zarablaan, I with my host of forty thousand valorous warriors who were both iron-hearted and high-spirited. My archers in practiced unison plucked their bowstrings and sent forth a deluge of poison-tipped shafts which showered down upon our foes. We were close enough to know that their aim was true, for we heard clearly the rising wails of fallen guards followed by desperate calls for reinforcements. By nightfall our catapults lobbed great torrents of fire, and sent them soaring over the wall to plunge mercilessly beyond, setting ablaze the heart of the city. Flames kept the dark desert night bright, and by dawn the sky was ashen from the soot of burning Zarablaan.

On the fourth day, we brought up the battering ram and made for the city gate. The fighting was the fiercest as nearer we drew, and arrows and spears and coals rained upon us. Many soldiers fell whilst they stood beside me, and the ground was so strewn with bodies that vultures from distant mountains filled the skies above, circling and cheering our folly with their shrill caws.

Stubbornly determined and wolfishly savage were the defenders of Zarablaan, but by the time the sun had its slow descent begun on the fifth and final day of our successful siege, I and my soldiers knew we soon would soon have our victory over the embattled city. No more could our foes repel our ruthless assaults, for their numbers were waning and their city slowly succumbed to our flames. Finally, the battering ram was successfully hauled into position, and finally, I dispatched the order that would secure the town--and our fates, one and all. Still I can hear it, echoing over and over: The pounding, the crashing, the thundering; that crushing roar as the great hammer collided repeatedly with the seemingly impregnable gate of Zarablaan. Finally, the wood cracked and split and splintered. The bolt groaned and snapped, and the braces bowed and failed as all gave way to explode into millions of fragments which tumbled and showered all over the sandy ground. And as the last sliver of that devastated gate came to rest upon the rubble, from my army arose a deafening cheer — a cry of ultimate conquest borne by dignity and allegiance. I, too, felt that call as it welled up from my lungs and ripped through my throat and screamed over my lips. Zarablaan was ours.

Through the gates and into the city marched my delbraths four, swords bloodied and spirits soaring. Fires yet burned, and some streets we found impassable for the debris in our path was thick. As darkness had come into bloom, I and my advisors thought it wise to hold the gate and advance no further till the dawn could illuminate our path; and so, after several days of battle, we were afforded one night of rest.

When again the sun rose, I had already hand-picked a hundred warriors with whom I would storm the city. All others, thought I, could remain behind to be called upon as I found necessary.

Down the narrow streets of conquered Zarablaan I stepped, leading the procession of one hundred soldiers. Through every aperture with care I looked, to the darkened end of each thin alley I gazed trying to catch a glimpse of a foe awaiting our final intrusion. Between high walls decorated by rows of cat-like faces, thirty on either side, and by red and black enameled tiles we were led as the road meandered through weird brick complexes. At each crossroads and corner, an altar was set, whereupon the wicked Zarablaanians must have long worshipped their hideous gods and offered up their own kind as sacrifices. The gray stone slabs hinted at the horrible rituals which had been performed upon them, and from them I sniffed the scent of blood and murder.

On either side, the buildings drew farther apart as the road widened. Into a sandy-carpeted courtyard stepped we servants of Zur Qumattai, where there before us rose up an enormous stepped tower which at once I knew must be set at the very core of Zarablaan. Fires blazed in great bowls set upon pedestals at its corners, and a thousand steps marked the single steep path toward its solitary and benighted doorway. Dozens of red and black banners symmetrically positioned about its base stewed listlessly on the foul-aired breath of the desert which snaked through these streets like a hungry stalking serpent.

This towering terraced monster of architecture was the central temple wherein our prize rested. I, and my men, eyed that place with such a sense of hatred I cannot say how it is that we did not tear it apart brick by brick just to revel in its destruction — but again, our emotions I know now were not our own.

And so up the steps we rallied, not taking time to question why not one single defender came from the shadows to challenge us; not wondering why the dead lay not in great numbers in the streets through which we had passed; not noticing that all the buildings save the great temple had been touched by fire. Blind and rage-driven, we raced forward. Forward, into the waiting arms of our own ruin, we charged.

Dark and dank were the chambers within the ziggurat of Zarablaan. We sped through narrow corridors, thrust firebrands into blackened cells to illuminate the stagnant shadows, and grimaced at the horrors we imagined once thrived within this foul temple. At length, we stumbled upon a great hall buried deep in the bowels of the place, and there we found the fabled Jewel of Kwilaleut. The much-hoarded treasure and sparkling gem of mystical properties rested before us upon a marble dais. Its sparkling surface captured the glimmering flames of our torches and redesigned them into a shimmering issuance that entranced both I and my soldiers. Our attentions were so diverted that each of us was taken aback when from the shadows leapt a single, ragged figure, eyes wild and lips drawn back in a savage snarl. He plunged screaming through the hall, a dagger firm in his clenched fist and held high.

I reacted poorly. My sword was scarcely out of its sheath when the madman was upon me. I could see the terror of my own eyes reflected in the smooth surface of the falling blade and I could hear the air rush as its keen edge hastened toward my chest.

Before the dagger could slice into my flesh, a spear sailed by me and caught the Zarablaanian in his gut. He staggered back, blood spurting out over his lips, and sank violently to the floor.

"How many others?" I demanded forcefully, kneeling at the fallen guardian's side.

"None," he whimpered, as tears sprang to his eyes. His chest shuddered and his breath grew more faint as moments raced by. "We have fought to the last man to keep the Jewel from the hands of others; we have failed. My sympathy to you and your countrymen is all I can offer."

"We burn your city and crush your armies and you offer us your pity?" I looked down inquisitively at the last Zarablaanian as he lay dying at my feet. When no response issued forth from his lips, I turned to my soldiers and smiled. I told them, "We have their Jewel, we have their souls and their swords, and now they offer us their sympathy as well—the Zarablaanians are a generous lot after all!"

Had I known that the Jewel was the Scourge of Zarablaan, I would not have taken the moment so lightly. A hearty round of laughter was shared by all, and soon we were leaving that horrible temple. I and my delbraths four soon departed fallen Zarablaan. We hauled with us back to Bel-ah'zund an abundance of spoils: Chests brimming with gold and silver pieces; diamonds of rare and exquisite beauty; precious gems and trinkets and baubles, charms and medallions and such. We claimed fine swords and axes and other weapons of war. But most important of all these things was the very Jewel of Kwilaleut.

During the days we spent returning to our homeland, I reflected upon the alleged properties of that strange gem that had so enchanted the zur. It troubled me that Zarablaan sat amidst a sea of wastes though the jewel promised fertility. It puzzled me that Zarablaan had not forged an empire as the jewel vowed that her armies would never fall on foreign soils. It frightened me that the jewel assured its bearers that death should not be feared, and yet not a single Zarablaanian survived our conquest.

Soon after our arrival in Bel-ah'zund, after the Jewel of Kwilaleut had been installed upon the crown of our victorious Zur Qumattai, I realized the nature of the plague I had brought upon our noble kingdom.

It occurred to me when wine and ales and food no longer enticed the masses. It occurred to me when strange howls filled the night skies of Bel-ah'zund, and shadows grew darker and more persistent even in the light of day.

When the first demons stalked our streets, I understood what had happened to poor Zarablaan.

Now, as the green fields encircling our city slowly wither and turn brown, I sit in the long shadows cast by a towering column of burnt-brick. I mourn the loss of the zur's flowering gardens, obliterated by a blight spread by those wicked things that serve that insidious jewel.

Our bellies are always full, and we are always ill.

Life here is now intolerable, yet escape is impossible. Those who have attempted to withdraw from the horrors of Bel-ah'zund have found it impossible. A ring of invisible fire sweeps around the city wall and prevents passage. Death is no more an option, for we cannot die by our own hands.

Now, we endure the scourge that has beset us, and we wait for an army to besiege our accursed city. When such an event happens, we shall welcome death under their swords; or, perhaps we shall fight like the noble Zarablaanians, trying to keep the poor fools from sharing our detestable fate.

The End

The Long Shelter
by
Denny E. Marshall

Jeremy moved into the house he grew up in after the older couple that lived there moved to Florida.

The last few nights, Jeremy swore he heard faint scratching or pounding from somewhere below. Like the couple that lived here before, Jeremy was hearing-impaired. He thought maybe it was his imagination or ringing in the ears. Still, it seemed so real.

The next night, Jeremy heard the sounds again and decided to investigate. He walked down the stairs to the basement. He listened but heard nothing. He sat and waited. After a few minutes, he heard a noise coming from below. He got as close to the sounds as possible. The sounds stopped. After many nights of trying to find out where the noises were coming from, Jeremy found a secret doorway.

Behind the door was a staircase. Jeremy heard the sounds coming from the bottom of the stairs.

He got a flashlight and walked down. There was a steel door. He heard someone say, "Help get me out of here, the inside door handle is broke."

Jeremy opened the door and saw an old man with a long beard. All this time alive in a well-stocked bomb shelter, when Jeremy thought his dad was dead.

The End

Skeletons of the Galaxy by Todd Hanks

Near the edge of Earth, the pirate ship
tossed and started sinking till it slipped
over the ledge and black, big sails unfurled.
Into the galaxy it left the world
to fly and float onto the face of space.
Crew of skinless men, the skeletons
swabbed the deck and tied the ropes like lace.

Haiku by Denny E. Marshall

small robots inside
need change from virus diet
turn into zombies

Little Sweetie
by
Marge Simon

She's a little sweetheart. Blue eyes bright, pinstriped tattoo patterns on her babyface. She probably got them for kicks at the start of the 21st century. She is ten thousand years old today, with most of the world's history behind her. What remains of the future is drawing closer to the end. Tired of growing up, she grows down, nestling in the unmarked graves of dead soldiers. You laugh and call me an old fool. Then come closer, my dear, see her there between those rotted skulls?

"Nonsense! What an adorable little girl! She's as alive as you and me," you say. "We must rescue her," you say.

Look at her closely. She's not asking for our help. We must leave now. Of course, you refuse to follow me, as I knew you would. See how she smiles at you? You think she's hungry for your love? Silly woman, look at those teeth!

The End

Baal-Tsephon by Lee Clark Zumpe

Osiris is slain, cut into pieces twice-seven,
leaving the pillars unguarded
Baal-Tsephon walks the sands
beneath a ragged moon shaving,
fingering a turquoise faience scarab
shadowless, he proliferates his hunger
among the hooded chosen
in the congested backstreets of Imbada slums
on the fringes of Cairo

Evergreen Terrace Apartment Review
by
Ron J. Cruz

The Evergreen Terrace Apartment Complex is a nice place to die. Okay, I can already imagine the apartment manager groaning about that sentence. He asked me to write an online review for Evergreen, which is silly since I am moving. But I want my deposit back, so I sit here drinking wine and writing this review. Let me start again.

As a single female 20-something, I feel comfortable saying the Evergreen Terrace Apartment Complex is a great place to live, nice place to die, but a terrible place to park. The bane of my existence, parking has been my one complaint since I got here. They do nothing about it. The assigned parking stalls have different numbers than the apartment units, to protect people supposedly, but it's a confusing mess of mismarked madness. Some people park wherever they want. Some of the only confrontations I have ever had in my life stemmed from parking here.

In fact, a parking miscue is how I met Emily, the tiny blue blossom. She was an indigo flower blooming on the side of a cactus. We could have been best friends, sisters, flickering eyes behind dark glasses, rubbing suntan lotion on each other's legs and shoulders by the pool. We could have been more. Our lips may have touched, skin may have kissed, all while sunrays danced on breezy ripples blown across clear water as we stretched out on soft beach towels. But no, she parked in my spot, and she did it several times!

The first time I was nice and addressed it. Emily rolled her eyes and gave a quasi-apology, mumbling about not realizing it was my spot. It pissed me off. I may have been upset; her idiot boyfriend looked me up and down and licked his teeth as he walked by. Okay, if I am being seriously honest, in retrospect, I may have just been irritated that she had a boyfriend. But the point is, her stupid little car did not belong in my private spot!

I do have to say the privacy afforded by these units is incredible. The walls have industrial-scale insulation as it never gets too hot in the summer, too cold in winter, and noises simply don't escape. For example, I am sure that nobody heard Emily's cries when my surgical strokes and glistening blades slowly slid into her. She wiggled and moaned at first, which made me smile. It was almost erotic, but hope left her eyes when she understood how it was going to end. My mom always said, "Hope dies last." She was a nurse, so she had probably witnessed it.

You cannot hear your neighbors, and your neighbors cannot hear you. When Emily screamed, I matched her volume. She got louder, I got louder, and then I collapsed on top of her laughing at the silliness of it all. Sometimes girls can get crazy, but she finally settled in, and we enjoyed a tender evening of candlelight and soft music. My tongue dancing along her tight skin, soft lips, and open wounds. I had a nice glass of Sangiovese I had been saving; I offered her some, she declined, but she might have caught the taste from my mouth.

I'm not sure how management screens the people for this apartment complex. Everyone seems nice, and everyone seems young, but everyone seems lacking in some way. That's not an "I'm better than everyone else," statement, just an observation from the people I've seen by the mailboxes, in the office, and around the grounds. I fear many couldn't pour beer from a boot if the instructions were written on the heel.

The doors in the Terrace are sturdy and secure, though painted in a hideous shade of green. When I knocked on Emily's door to confront her again about her using my parking spot, my fist thundered but the door didn't budge. The peephole needs improvement, though. When people peek out, the light goes dark. There is no retreating down the hall at that point, not that Emily would.

She was a petite girl with a long, thin neck and large, round breasts that filled and stretched her t-shirts. She had a hummingbird tattoo behind her ear that was visible when she wore her hair back. In the face of my anger, her boyfriend came out and moved her car. He didn't seem as interested in me that night.

That spectacular burst of anger should have settled it. Don't park in my spot! I will pound on the door and scream! But it seemed to have developed into a routine, and each time I was angrier and she cared less. They had to be toying with me. The last time it happened, she opened the door and leaned in the frame, and dopey came bouncing down the hall. He smiled, allowed himself to dance in the air before me, donned striped boxers, and went out to move the car.

It was raining as I pulled my car into my spot, watching him smirk as he ran back up the stairs. It could never happen again. Something had to be done. I mean, what would you do?

The closets in the units are spectacular. Seriously nice. The walk-in closet in the master bedroom has enough room for a couple of shoe racks and a stool to sit on while lacing them up. If you remove those, however, there is also enough room to lay a sheet of plastic out and play with a neighbor as she bleeds out. I am not sure what exercises Emily did, perhaps just blessed with great genes, but I appreciate them. I'm guessing yoga. She laid there, whimpering, cold, and scared. I flicked her panties and bra away with a scalpel. They seemed to want to come off, springing away from her body. But why is it women don't even bother trying to match their panties and bra? She had a tight white, lacy affair of silk stretched across her hips, but a messy heap of padded pinkness covering her deep breasts. It's the little things that bug me. But this is supposed to be about the apartments.

The bathrooms are extremely confident. The showers haven't been codified with eco-friendly nozzles, so you can still get amazingly adequate pressure from them, and if you keep them clean, even half-assedly, blood rolls through the drain without a stain. I removed Emily's elegant long fingers, small hands, and fertile feet there. Again, the insulation for noise is exquisite. There is enough elbow room to get into the task at hand, even if that's sawing and cutting. Our skin-to-skin time in the tub, beneath a steady stream of warm water, was the memory of Emily I will hold forever. She gasped and choked while I pressed into her, dipping into the moist pocket of her soul. I inhaled every last breath that leaked from her mouth, devolving to small whispers.

I think the best thing about living in the Evergreen apartment complex is that you can pretty much throw anything in the dumpster. I've seen people that don't even live here drop off mattresses, furniture, and even things you're not supposed to throw away like televisions or computer monitors. And there is shopping within walking distance.

I found a green seabag at the thrift store two blocks away. Plastic bags inside garbage bags inside a navy grade seabag: perfect, leakproof container for Emily now that she had gone to pieces on me. Emily, with her toned limbs, pierced belly button, high cheeks, and that indifferent expression of satisfaction she wore on her thick lips, and yet her remains were picked up like any other shit thrown into a dumpster. If nothing else, America is proficient at taking out the trash.

This is a review of the apartments, and I keep getting away from it. The carpets are soft and durable. I'm not sure what they treat them with, but I think it's impossible to damage them. It must be some type of stain repellant on steroids; before our final interlude, severed Emily crawled like a snail, leaving a bloody trail from the bathroom to the front door. All the while, I was stretched out, napping on the couch. She stained the wall and the door fumbling for the handle, which finally woke me up. I doubled the mess dragging her thrashing ass back. I was sure I'd ruined the carpet, but it cleaned up with towels and vinegar. The carpets must have amazingly resilient padding below them.

Evergreen Terrace Apartments! Move in. They are great! There will be units available very soon. I am moving out, Emily already left, and I don't think her boyfriend technically lived there. So, come take a tour! I can't rave enough about their quality.

You might think I'm careless to leave a review like this online, but I want you to know how amazing these apartments are. Besides, Emily might not have even been her real name. And maybe I'm talking about the Evergreen's sister property. Shit, who knows, I might have made the whole thing up. People disappear all the time, especially the ones who irritate me. Poof.

The apartment manager doesn't even know my real name or hair color, and he keeps his sliding glass door open at night. Perhaps he likes the breeze off the delta when he's sleeping. He's certainly not as concerned about his security as he should be. If you're thinking about living here, I guess that it will be under new management soon. He should have listened to the resident's concerns, like parking and shit. Maybe the new management will.

Be kind … this is my first review! I do believe it's a beautiful place to live. I would stay here forever, but my tomato plants just do not get enough light on the balcony. I can't get them to grow, so I am moving.

If the sun in your neighborhood is good, who knows? Maybe I will be your neighbor.

The End

Centennial
by
Lee Clark Zumpe

Mason Willetts grunted as his eyes opened and the dream he had been having disintegrated. For a few frightening moments, the blurry images from sleep lingered, and the older man struggled to discern reality from fantasy. Age had dulled his wits, occasionally depriving him of the dignity of intellect. He could not form words to describe what he had been imagining; he could not even assemble thoughts into logical patterns.

He had dozed off while watching reruns.

"Y'alright in there, Mason?" Alice Mae could hear the old man coughing in the parlor, unsuccessfully trying to clear a lifetime of cigarette smoke from his ragged lungs. "Today ain't gonna be your day, is it? I hear there's a parade passing our way 'round noontime."

"Noisy raucous they'll make," Mason said, muttering into a kerchief. His eyes fluttered as he tried to focus on the television set. He had seen this particular episode of *Bonanza* a dozen times. Much to his chagrin, the remote had vanished into the great abyss between the seat cushion and the armrest. The glass of sweet tea Alice Mae had poured for him rested on the edge of the end table, leaching condensation onto a white doily. "What need have we for a parade on this awful day?"

"Why Mason," Alice Mae said, although he hadn't intended for her to hear the question. "Don't you know that today is Founder's Day? It was exactly 100 years ago today that Yonah came into being."

The little town sat along Panther Creek just upstream from where it emptied into the French Broad River. Looming overhead to the south was Misery Mountain, where history claimed a regiment of Confederate soldiers had been massacred following their surrender at the close of the War of Northern Aggression, as the locals still referred to it. Townsfolk had erected a monument to them, which attracted fewer visitors with each passing year. Creeping vines had begun to weave their way around its base as it towered over Oconee bells in a hemlock stand.

"Is that right?" Mason patted his forehead with the kerchief, sopping up summer sweat. He raised his right hand and looked at the intricate white scars all but hidden beneath the tan, leathery flesh. The interlaced scores on his palm burned anew as he traced their form – throbbing just like the day the blade etched the cryptic symbols into his trembling hand. The memory of that day still made him shudder. "I thought there was something strange in the air this morning. Last night, I dreamt of things I haven't had reason to recollect in many years."

"This city's catching up with you, old man." Alice Mae peered in through the parted curtains, through the dirty screen. "Ain't been that long since you turned 100, has it?"

"It's been a while, ma'am," Mason said, shaking his head. He routinely claimed to be between 105 and 120 years old, depending on what day of the week someone questioned him. Having been adopted as a child, he could never be sure of his exact age. "Near as I can speculate," he said – a phrase he always used to preface his questionable estimations – "I must be about to turn 112 come December."

"Well, sir, if that is so," Alice Mae said, her gaze now fixed on her Southern gothic novel, "and you have lived in Yonah most of your life, then you must remember what it was like when the town was founded."

"That I do, Miss Alice; that I do."

Gradually, he leaned forward and pushed himself off the edge of the easy chair. At his age, standing meant taking inventory of every aching bone, every stiff joint, every atrophied muscle. Crossing the cluttered room, he scowled at the framed photographs crowding the top of an antique desk, collected and arranged by his wife before her death. Their sons and daughters had all moved far away from the quiet North Carolina community and only occasionally returned when funerals beckoned them.

Mason wondered which of his estranged offspring would bother to attend his interment.

****

Across town, Perry Sellers shuffled across the carpeted floor of his private quarters at the Freedom Colony Assisted Living Facility. The establishment's oldest continuous resident, Perry spent most mornings lounging in comfortable slippers and a bathrobe watching old movies on a small television set. The remnants of breakfast remained on the kitchenette – a slice of orange, a piece of toast that had been nibbled into a crescent, a lump of bland scrambled eggs dappled with pepper. His doctors would not allow him the extravagance of salt. The morning's newspaper stretched across the table, its headlines ignored. Perry had given up on the news. Only the obituaries interested him at this late stage of the game.

One day soon, he expected to see his name on that page of trivial tragedies, his life summed up in impartial and dispassionate bullets composed by conceited custodians of the recently expired.

This morning, though, one front page notation had caught his attention. Picturesque Yonah would celebrate its 100th birthday with a parade and festival and fireworks beneath the stars. The centennial commemoration, according to the acting town council, would recall the town's humble beginnings, honor its many achievements, and recognize its pastoral heritage.

The community's skeletons, however, would presumably remain veiled behind a century of deftly crafted duplicity and deception.

Most municipalities secreted the inconvenient stains of past iniquities and suppressed the sordid indignities upon which their foundations had been laid. History abounded with festering wounds, the censored sins of previous generations prematurely forgiven and forgotten. Perry knew about Yonah's dark past and had played an active role in keeping it concealed for all these years.

As a member of one of Yonah's founding families, Perry had spent his adult life fighting to preserve the town's charm and affability. Likewise, he stifled sporadic chatter describing deals with Appalachian witches and midnight negotiations with a forgotten mountain tribe who worshipped ancient gods.

Any mention of shadowmen lurking through the deep forests met with fanatical scorn and mockery.

"Mr. Sellers," a nurse Angelina said, poking her head through the front door. Freedom Colony did not always count personal privacy among its top features. "Sorry to disturb you, sir, but you must not have heard me knocking." At least the woman kept her gaze fixed on the floor in case Perry had not finished dressing. "I just wanted to remind you that the bus will be leaving in three-quarters of an hour."

"Bus?" Perry rarely kept track of the facility's innumerable field trips. Outings to movie theaters, shopping malls, and stage shows attracted many residents, offering them an escape from the monotony of daily bingo tournaments, square dances, and Scrabble contests in the inadequately stocked game room. "Where are the sheep off to today?" Perry considered the excursions pointless and pitiful, particularly the insipid conversations initiated by the activities director during the bus ride. "Cherokee for some blackjack? Maggie Valley for a clogging show?"

"Of course not," the nurse said, opening the door wider. She gathered his dirty plates, swept the food into a garbage can, and checked to make sure he had taken his morning medicine. "You know today is Founder's Day. We're going down to the football field to watch the parade and fireworks. There'll be hotdogs and popcorn."

"Football field? That's only a couple blocks from here. What do we need a bus for?"

"Not all of our residents are as physically active as you are, Mr. Sellers." Angelina smiled. For a man nearing his 108th birthday, Perry's health could not have been better. Mild hypertension and insomnia had plagued him for 25 years, but otherwise, he remained a model of fitness, walking several miles a day and keeping slim and energetic. "Some people aren't so lucky."

"Luck has nothing to do with it." Perry scowled. "It's a combination of exercise, diet, and chronic cynicism."

"So am I take it you won't be joining us?"

"If I decide to go," Perry said, rising from the sofa. His bathrobe, loosely fastened, parted in the middle, revealing more of his anatomy than the nurse cared to survey. "I'm quite capable of getting there on my own."

Angelina scurried from the room without another word, miffed but not surprised by Perry's wanton disrespect. He had developed a reputation at Freedom Colony as the most uncouth resident, quick to criticize every program, every mandate, and every new staff member. Still, his place there *remained* secure – his endowment had funded the entire institution.

His contempt for his neighbors, his doctors, and the workers whose efforts made life at Freedom Colony bearable for most dwellers reflected his shame.

Perry clenched his fist, fingernails biting into his palm. The old scars stung, reminding him of the pain and grief and blood. Opening his hand, he saw the cursed symbols as if for the first time. Each convoluted icon, each meticulously formed character defied translation. Though the injury had faded over the years, though the script remained a mystery to him, Perry understood its significance all too well. He understood the magnitude of the covenant, and he knew that the pact made a century earlier would expire on this day.

As he dressed, Perry dredged up images of a meeting that took place beneath a sky full of foreboding stars in a clearing surrounded by shadow-haunted forests. A dozen families, eager to establish a farming community, had traveled from the small seaport town Smithville on the Carolina coast to an isolated corner of the highlands. Though they had already acquired the right to settle, they discovered upon their arrival the descendants of a lost Scottish colony living in the wilds of the Appalachian forests. Culture and custom had essentially been bled from them by long centuries living isolated from the outside world, and in desperation, they had reverted to savage ways and the worship of old gods. With Beltane fires blazing atop surrounding summits, the settlers struck a bargain that ensured their claim on the valley and provided for their well-being for a limited time.

A chilling scream stirred the old man from his dark memories, sent him dashing into the corridor. Death frequented Freedom Colony, most often quietly and late at night. Nurses and other attendants had become accustomed to finding patients motionless and unresponsive in their beds, victims of strokes or heart attacks or aneurisms. Still, none of them expected the grisly scenes they would encounter that day – none of them expected the blood, the brutality, and the brazen debauchery.

History's long shadows had finally fallen over Yonah.

****

Yonah residents gathered along Main Street, muttered muted protests upon learning of the parade's cancellation. Law enforcement officials oversaw an orderly evacuation of the sidewalks as officials asked for order and composure.

"We'd like everyone to go home and to remain inside for the rest of the afternoon," a voice said through a distant loudspeaker. "We apologize for the inconvenience this has caused, but we've had to divert our resources to other matters today. I'm sure that the local news station will be reporting the story, so at this time, we ask that everyone calmly clear the streets."

Several blocks from Main Street, Mason stood on the edge of his porch, watching neighbors anxiously streaming along the sidewalks. Their silence reflected a dormant fear blossoming among them – an innate despair that had plagued them for generations. They marched swiftly, steadily, obediently toward their homes without further complaint as dread settled across the valley.

Sirens wailed across the city blocks, speeding toward desperate pleas for help. Soon, the police would be overwhelmed by the situation and would become bogged down in counting bodies and coping with the appalling atrocities.

Alice Mae had left following a frantic call from one of her daughters. She promised to contact the church, to make sure someone would stop by and make a meal for Mason that evening. Mason had nodded and offered his condolences, though at the time, she did not understand his premature sympathy. He knew the horrors that awaited her.

Mason waited for the crowds to subside. By midday, the abandoned pavement stretched toward the encircling mountains, the sidewalks and well-manicured lawns longed for the laughter of children, and the town's populace congregated around television sets watching the unfolding mayhem. National news networks had already picked up on the story, and helicopters from Asheville and Franklin circled overhead.

According to sketchy reports, twenty victims had been recovered throughout the town, each badly mutilated and defiled. State police and National Guard units had been summoned to the site of the grisly murders, but officials could not yet identify a suspect in the killings.

Mason shambled along the vacated streets, stopping to rest briefly at each intersection. His declining health frustrated him. He cursed his arthritic limbs, his aching joints, and his struggling heart. Still, he had survived. So far as he knew, he might well be the only one left living. In all, 13 children had been marked that night to seal the covenant that effectively eliminated the wild Scottish clan and guaranteed a century of comfort and prosperity.

Though Mason had not been directly involved in ironing out the details, he recognized the unscrupulousness with which the founders had fashioned the accord. Civilized or savage, the forest folk did not deserve the fate their gods consigned to them.

The football field where the local high school played Friday night games had been situated on a patch of ground formerly known as Willetts' Bald, named after Mason's father, Wilbur Willetts. The 13 tall, gray sculpted stones which once sat amidst the grassy field had been removed and deposited along the steep, forested slopes enveloping the town. Yonah's founders had meticulously erased the runes scrawled across the mossy surface of each rock, defacing history and eradicating all evidence of the land's former inhabitants.

As Mason reached the gate, he scanned the field, expecting to find it vacant. To his surprise, his eyes fixed on one lone figure seated in the bleachers – a man he could identify even at a distance.

"We're the only ones," Perry said as he watched Mason approaching. The skies had turned black and icy. Unseasonably cold winds scoured the valley as if trying to purge the region of its hereditary culpability. "I wasn't even sure if you were still alive. It's been a long time."

"Too long," Mason agreed, embracing his old friend. "I'm sorry that it took this to reunite us."

"I had almost convinced myself it had all been a dream." Perry held out his hand, revealing his scarred palm. The symbols had become inflamed and seeped blood. "So long ago, like a nightmare diminished by dawn. Only, the signs always came back to haunt me."

"You've seen the shadowmen?"

"They've been with us all along, biding their time, waiting to slaughter as they had originally intended." The gods with whom their ancestors had bargained had not exterminated their former adherents. Instead, the clan had been forcibly displaced to an alternate and less hospitable dimension. The boundary between the parallel worlds remained tenuous and allowed the victimized exiles sporadic access in incorporeal form. "Our time is up, and our children must answer for our sins."

"It was all in vain, then,"

"Not necessarily." Perry raised his palm to the dusky, sinister skies. "So long as we survive, they are obliged to offer an extension of the contract."

"And they're aware of this?"

"They're just waiting to see if we've remembered."

In the middle of the field, a flash of light erupted into a dancing flame. From the blaze emerged a tall, willowy, wan gentleman wearing a vintage flat black suit consisting of matching coat, vest, and slacks, an Edwardian white shirt, and a beaver top hat. Where shoes would have been, cloven hooves dug into the yielding loam.

Perry and Mason recognized him immediately as the mediator with whom the settlers had negotiated.

"Pity you've survived," the intermediary said, clutching the parchment that bore the signatures of Yonah's founders. "I would have thought a hundred years would see you all neatly into your graves."

"Longevity runs in my family," Perry said. "We've been waiting for this day, waiting to set things right."

"There's no setting things right, gentlemen. The terms of the agreement were clear: Your fathers agreed to lease this land for 100 years. You have had your century, but you have failed to live up to the terms provided for in the covenant." The intermediary unfurled the yellowed scroll revealing the intricacies of the settlement, traced the scrawled script with a grimy, bony finger as his lips mouthed unintelligible words. Finally, he continued. "Your fathers offered us blood sacrifices and swore their devotion – yet not one amongst you offers tribute to us now; not one shrine has been erected in our honor, and no blood flows upon this field where souls were once surrendered to appease us. I see no reason to delay the return of our former worshippers, whose devotion to us was never lacking."

"Fine, fine," Perry said, shaking his head in contempt. "You do that – you summon up your shadowmen, let them have their fill of vengeance until everyone in this town is dead. Let the slaughter continue until Panther Creek runs red with blood like it did when they butchered those poor Confederate soldiers on Misery Mountain."

"Perry," Mason thumped his hand against his old friend's chest, cautioning him. "What are you doing? We're supposed to be renegotiating the covenant…"

"No more covenant, no more pledges and vows of fidelity," Perry brushed Mason's arm aside. "If these gods are so eager to return to blind faith and unsophisticated reverence, let them. I would have thought they could have seen the benefits of more a more cultured, less uncivilized form of devotion."

"Explain yourself," the intermediary said. Behind him, shadowmen had begun assembling, their indistinct forms growing more tangible with each passing moment. Out across Yonah, the initial carnage had been suspended as members of the displaced clan rallied to the center of the vortex spiraling in dark, grim clouds above the football field. "If you have sufficient cause, speak now."

"After settling here, Mason's father started a lumber business. From logging camps on the opposite side of Misery Mountain, he cleared thousands of acres before the federal government came in and bought up the land – he helped provide the infrastructure Yonah needed. My daddy," Perry said, a proud smile erupting on his withered face, "He built the first factories in this part of the Appalachians. He took the people of Yonah off their fields and their farms and put them to work."

"How does this affect our covenant?"

"Those factories produced guns – all kinds of guns. Rifles, sidearms, machine guns for the two world wars. Later on, the company diversified. The people of Yonah started making guidance components for air-to-air missiles and trigger mechanisms for nuclear warheads." Perry paused, scowled. His momentary pride shriveled as he recalled the point of his argument and shame resurfaced gnawing at his soul. The realization of the suffering for which his father, his company, and he had been responsible made him wince and shudder. "Tell me," he said, staggering. "Tell me how much blood this town has shed over the last century. This town has shouldered that guilt, built a religion around it. Compare that to the insignificant sacrifices and offerings your uncivilized clan once provided you and tell me whose devotion you prefer."

Silence followed as the intermediary considered Perry's argument. The swirling clouds thickened as dusk plunged the town into complete darkness. Along the hilltops surrounding the community, fires flickered into being. Overhead, unfamiliar stars shimmered in the eye of the vortex.

"I have conferred with those with whom this contract was initially forged. It is their observation that civilization accompanied by technology and apathy contribute more to the cause of chaos than generations of primitive sacrifices."

"So we will be able to extend the contract and keep our land?"

"There is no need," the intermediary said, shaking his head. "You have paid in full with the souls of countless millions over the last century. The land is yours. Do with it as you will."

At that instant, the shadowmen, enraged by the second betrayal, lunged toward the intermediary. In a blinding flash, both their pathetic displaced souls and the messenger of the ancient gods vanished. The contract, now concluded, remained as a reminder of past sins to the townsfolk of Yonah.

Perry clutched his chest, collapsed to his knees.

"It's over," he said, leaning forward against the railing overlooking the football field. Across the town, street lamps began to glow. The nightmare had come to an end. "Listen, Mason…"

"Be quiet, old man. I'll get an ambulance."

"No time – go to my room at Freedom Colony. In the nightstand by the bed, in the top drawer, there's a sealed envelope. Deliver it to my lawyer – his address is on the outside. It's important. You have to promise…"

"Of course, I'll take care of it. Now lean back, let me find some help…"

For Perry, the night grew darker and colder, its grasp undeniable. He watched his old friend shuffle off in search of assistance, watched as the stars above Yonah emerged from the dissipating clouds. Without dark forces demanding appeasement, without quotas to be reached, and wicked whims to be satiated, Yonah, he prayed, would have an optimistic future not tainted by indignity and infamy.

With Perry's passing, the shame would fade into history.

****

YONAH – The death of Perry Sellers, longtime chairman of the military contractor Sellers Industries, has triggered a complete reorganization of the firm. Sellers, who still owned a controlling share in the company, left explicit instructions to restructure the business and retrofit its 27 factories worldwide. Under the new name Yonah Founders Ltd., the company will terminate the manufacturing of weapons and weapons components to focus on building affordable prefabricated homes for developing countries.

The End

A Shadow in the Night
by
Colleen M. Farrelly

A dew had fallen on the outskirts of town while I wandered the forest, pondering my predicament and hugging my coat close in the midnight chill. The air was still. Few critters stirred as I disturbed the underbrush; those awoken scuttled into the shrubbery abutting the footpath.

Fog veiled the valley and its villages, a soft blanket on a cold night. Shrouded in mist, a white shadow perched atop a hill, nestled among the oaks, moaning and groaning in the night. Did the shadow share my sorrow?

I pass her cottage on the outskirts of town—silent now, save the snore of a half-drunken stupor. Her fender still has the dents from her last bender, the blood still kissing the cracked windshield—his blood. I wonder if he suffered.

a broken window

and my knife—

a banshee in the night

The Sacrificial Girl
by
Matthew Wilson

Even in my old age, I curse my compassion.

I was young when the witch hunters wished to throw my friend into the fire. Mother said love was not for me, but Sally was kind; her herbs saved me from the plague, but the villagers feared her magic.

When famine festered through the fields, they sought a cause rather than a cure and decided on a sacrifice.

I waited till her captors got drunk in celebration, singing songs about the great fire they'd build in the morning before I crept into the old barn and cut her bonds with my dagger.

Mother was wrong; now, Sally and I would flee into the hills and make a new life together.

Buy Sally did not forgive past transgression so easily.

I couldn't go near her when she summoned lightning from the sky and opened the cracking earth to great lakes of lava that swallowed up the thatched houses of sleeping children.

By morning, only a lake of bubbling fire remained where our village had stood. Sated, Sally told me she was ready to move on, to start over now she had killed a thousand fools.

I ran from her and had been running all my life. God, I have lived too long with a guilty conscious, continually changing my name and town so she will not find me. I've seen firsthand what she does to those who anger her.

But my mother was right. Love is not for me. All that keeps me company are nightmares of smoke in my lungs and grinning faces watching from the window. Even after all these years of telling myself I am done with witches, I do not think they are done with me.

God damn an old fool's compassion.

The End

The Lovers by Marge Simon

Oh, lordy, how they do love!
once turned, and turned together
in an exclusive vampire orgy
that is only for the chosen ones --

love takes on a whole new meaning

Where shall we dine tonight?
Stefan asks his raven-haired bride,
knowing well what she will say,
laughter in her azure eyes --

love takes on a whole new meaning

When the weekend parties end,
a man walks down a darkened street,
a little tipsy from a one-night stand,
that's the best time for encounters --

and love takes on a whole new meaning.

The Curious Case of the Bookshop in Brighton
by
Francis-Marie de Châtillon.

Harry Fielding was a happy man. His messy divorce now finalised, he could get on with the rest of his life, which, he reasoned, at 45 left him quite a few years ahead. He'd gotten out of London and away from the secondary school where he taught, and moved to Brighton at the beginning of the month. Harry was still exploring the details of Brighton and Hove (hated the Royal Pavilion) and the various watering-holes for which it was famous (loved the Great Eastern). Harry had managed to come out of his divorce with enough money in the bank to buy a small, Victorian-terraced house in Cuthbert Road, in the Queen's Park area, up near the hospital. He loved it. There was a corner shop almost across the road and a pub at the end, which, happily for him, wasn't noisy at chuck-out time on Fridays and Saturdays. He planned to do a bit of redecorating just to put his mark on it, so to speak. With this in mind, Harry was out-and-about this Saturday morning looking to buy a few inexpensive things for his home.

The sun shone brightly this late April morning as Harry strolled into the Lanes, that narrow, winding system of passages that used to be the centre of the old fishing town of Brighthelmstone, to explore some of the quaint sites there. He stopped at a pawnbroker to examine some second-hand signet rings, something he wanted to get for his right hand, now that he'd taken off his wedding ring of nearly twenty years. He browsed in two or three bookshops; he had taken a keen interest in reading now, rather than spend the evening sprawled in front of the television. Afterward, he had a coffee in a small café before moving on to the antique shops and 'curiosity' shops that abound.

Turning into one lane, he found what looked to be a strange shop. The front windows were yellow as if someone had covered them old cellophane years ago to stop things from fading in the window. The windows were also well below eye level, which indicated to Harry that it was a basement, yet it had no upper parts. It looked old, with an odd entrance that made him go up four or five steps only to descend again when inside.

The shop interior was a veritable Aladdin's cave of old leather-bound volumes, antique mirrors, paintings, and whatnot else. Everything was dusty. The light was dim, and the recesses of the room quite dark. Chaos seemed to be the order of the day. To his surprise, there appeared to be nobody attending the shop. He called out to announce himself, but no one answered or came to attend him. Harry felt a little uncomfortable looking around, seemingly alone. Still, he shifted about in the gloom finding old silver teapots piled up in one corner, along with goblets of varying shapes and sizes. Then, he moved on to some ancient Venetian mirrors. At these, he contemplated whether one of the larger ones would suit in the living room; but then dismissed it, as seeing himself too often would make him feel a glutton for punishment.

He saw vast piles of what looked like mixed art-work: canvases of all sizes with and without frames, prints, and drawings likewise stacked against a wall. Now, these interested Harry as he was looking for things to hang on his walls, and so he set to amongst them. He went through dozens, but strangely, nothing caught his eye. Harry was about to turn away and give up, when the corner of a small panel painting, about 10 x 8 inches, caught his eye. He pulled it out from under a couple of prints and studied it.

It was a small portrait of a stately-looking elderly man in Renaissance-styled clothing. He was obviously wealthy and, although almost square to the picture-plane, appeared to be eyeing someone over to his left, engaging their attention. Harry liked the portrait, and he put it aside. He then noticed there was another small picture again mostly hidden amongst other material, and so he tugged that out also. He smiled broadly. It was another fine-looking panel portrait, about the same size as the other; only this was of a younger man in his mid-fifties. He, too, looked authoritative and commanding in his aspect and attire; Harry put the portrait down with the other.

Seconds later, a man appeared from out of nowhere. Startled, Harry jumped; the man had, seemingly, materialised in the manner of Jeeves in one of Wodehouse's books. Seeing Harry jump, he sort of bounced backward.

"Oh! I'm so sorry to have come on you so suddenly, please forgive me!" the man apologised.

Harry smiled back, weakly. He was looking into the visage of a small, almost wizened man, whose face was crazed with lines. In contrast to his frame, his face was plump, with two very prominent buccal fat pads, which accentuated his deep nasolabial creases. Harry thought this chap was eyeing him pretty much as a man might a juicy steak after a fast.

"Are you the owner?" Harry asked, at last, pushing aside his thoughts.

"Oh, yes. Indeed, dear sir!" he fired back with evident enthusiasm. He held his hand out in greeting. Harry took it, and to his surprise, received a firm and vigorous handshake.

"Well, can I ask you about these two portraits here?" Harry held them up. "Do you know who the artist might be, by any chance?"

"Ahhhhh now," the elderly gentleman let out. "These are two excellent pieces, of course. Who the artist is or the sitters, however, I'm afraid I don't know. I bought them at auction, and the auction house was also at a loss to identify them." At this, he beamed wistfully. Harry thought him a bizarre old bird.

"What price is on them, Mr...." His voice trailed off, yet the old man did not supply a name, but just eyed him with his head tilted to one side. "Because I'm interested in buying them for my house. I've just moved here, you see." Why Harry supplied the last intelligence, he had no idea.

"Oh, my dear man, congratulations! Con-grat-u-lations!" he cried grandly. Harry found this almost comical and wondered if the man's bowtie would start spinning like an airscrew on a Spitfire; then, as if pulled by one, the old man shot forward and slapped Harry on the back a couple of times.

"Er, thanks," Harry said, surprised. He looked and felt like a confounded Pharisee.

"Now, the price! Yeeees, price." The old man looked thoughtful for a moment and then cried out theatrically, "Let's say £5 each! Yes, I say, £5 for the two!"

Harry thought, *this guy's nuts.*

Despite the bargain being well in his favour, Harry tried to explain he couldn't possibly pay so little, but the eccentric old gentleman wouldn't hear of it; he was practically pressing Harry to take them.

"Think of it as a small welcoming gift to our town, young man!" Again, Harry thought, *yep, this guy's seriously nuts!*

Harry paid the £5, again protesting the smallness of the sum. In return, as if prepared beforehand, the strange old man produced a receipt of almost A4 size written in what looked like copperplate. The man thanked Harry profusely, pumped his hand vigorously and all but danced for joy about the shop. Harry didn't pretend to understand this queer old man and his eccentric manner — he was just glad he'd got the pictures. Harry left the shop, a contented man. On the way home, he made a small detour to Trafalgar Street to sink a pint in the Eastern, and then another near his house at the Cuthbert. As he downed the second, he thought, *that old man seemed pretty pleased to be rid of those paintings — hope they're not stolen goods!*

****

At home, he contemplated the room the paintings would look their best and decided on his bedroom on the wall at the foot of his bed. He reasoned that he could sit up and look at them as he read his books before sleeping.

Harry measured out the height and distance apart for the two paintings and knocked a couple of masonry nails into the wall. He placed the portraits, so it appeared the elderly man looking to his left was engaging the other slightly younger man. Harry felt most pleased with this small creative touch. That night, he again popped out to the pub and then ordered an Indian takeaway. He watched about 30 minutes of some banal television programme before he decided that his bed called.

He wearily climbed the stairs and, after a quick trip to the bathroom, slipped on his PJs, and got under the quilt. He sat pondering the two pictures before him. Who were they? What lives had they had? Were they even real people, or did they only exist in the imagination of the artist? The last, he hoped, was not the case; he preferred a real backstory to his new purchases. Harry was reading *The Thirty-Nine Steps* at the moment — he was about halfway through — and he loved it! Reading was far better than the TV. Soon, his eyes closed, the *Steps* slid from his hand, and Harry slept.

Part Two

There was a loud noise. It had come from somewhere in the street. Sitting up smartly, Harry listened then checked his watch. It was nearly 3:00 a.m., so it couldn't have been some pisshead from the pub. He wondered about an intruder somewhere, then dismissed the thought — intruders tend to be quiet. After a few minutes listening, the street being again silent, he turned over. He tried to sleep, cursing whatever it was that had woken him.

As he lay, he thought he heard faint whisperings; straining his ears hard, he wondered what it could be. He could swear there was something, but it was just out of reach. What on earth was it? Maybe it was just a figment of his imagination brought on by the startling noise. He tried to sleep but quite in vain, as the ever-so-slight whisperings continued. "This is quite maddening!" he said aloud, and throwing his legs out of bed, he jumped up.

He made some tea in the kitchen, hoping it would relax him and aid his return to sleep. Harry noticed that down here, the strange whispering had stopped. He went into the living room, which was at the front of the house, like his bedroom, and listened. There was nothing. He opened the front door and peered out; only an empty street greeted him.

He drank his tea and went upstairs and tried to settle. He turned off the bedside light, but not even a minute passed before the whispering started again. This time they were more audible, but he couldn't make out what was being said.

"Sod this nonsense!" Harry cried. He sprang up again, and grabbing the golf club he wisely or unwisely kept by the bed (his ex-wife had seriously mixed feelings about this habit as a security measure), he flew down the stairs, determined to confront whoever the bastards were that interfered with his rest.

He flung the front door open, strode out into the garden, and looked around. Checking the street and around the house, he found nothing. Harry decided they were hiding.

Whacking the club on the path, Harry shouted, "Okay, you fuckers. Come out. Now!" But no one materialised from anywhere. He waited, then shouted again, whacking the club a second time. Yet, still nothing.

"Well, whoever you are, you'd better piss off quick, or I'll call the police to you. See if I fucking don't, you arseholes!" Frustrated, he went inside. He wondered if he'd woken the neighbours.

For the second time, Harry climbed the stairs to try and sleep. He was frustrated. "It's enough to make a monk wank," he said to himself. As he entered the bedroom again, he thought he heard something; but this time, he just thought, *fuck it*, and jumped under the quilt. This time, Harry was soon asleep.

He was in the throes of a terrible dream. Harry was revolving about in the bed like a top, his pyjamas damp with perspiration. Rain was pouring down somewhere, and a frightful wind was howling around the house. Just above the noise, Harry could hear arguing and shouting. He woke with a start, gasping for breath. To his amazement, the weather had changed dramatically from earlier, and the storm of his dream was real. He realised that he must have somehow imported it into his sleep, and he shivered despite being hot. Harry padded to the bathroom opposite his bedroom and shaking off his PJs, he turned on the water to freshen himself. Harry was just soaping himself over in the shower when, through the hiss of water, he heard it: a low, anguished moan, slow as pouring treacle, came from somewhere very near to him. Then:

"You killed him. Murderers! Oh, murderers all, you accursed family." This was followed by another long stomach-wrenching moan of grief.

Harry stood statue-still, fearing some lunatic intruder. Staring through the steam and involuntarily holding his breath, he watched to see if the door handle would turn. He hadn't locked the door and felt like bolting over to secure it to improvise a sort of safe room.

"All your grasping family deserve to die, Piero de' Medici. It's a shame and a pity only Giuliano met his fate that day." The voice was rasping and harsh. "Bernardo and my nephew, Francesco, could only do half the task with the knife, for they couldn't kill your Lorenzo. Those inept priests are to blame for that, curse them! "

"You are a pig, Jacopo de' Pazzi!" He snapped. "Ahhh, but look what honeyed vengeance we took on your family," he cried with relish. "You: hanged from the Palazzo Vecchio along with the decomposing Archbishop Salviati — the bastard who plotted with you all. Your precious Francesco de' Pazzi: hanged! And that cur Bernado Baroncelli." The voice let out a bitter laugh.

The voices wore on at each other in similar vein, one accusing the other. The one Jacopo was given grisly treatment: buried in some church, he was later dug up and dragged through the streets. Buried again, he was apparently disinterred a second time and propped up by children against the door of his house. His rotting skull was used as a macabre door-knocker. Harry listened and wondered if he was having some psychiatric interlude. He felt like his legs might give way.

Then, as if a radio had been switched off, the voices went silent; in fact, Harry thought it must be a radio programme. Now, the gruesome dialogue had stopped. Vivifying himself, so to speak, he jumped out the shower, wrapped a towel round him, and went to the bedroom. He stopped dead. Harry looked at the pictures disbelievingly: where they had been square to the wall minutes before, they were now tilted at crazy angles. "How the...?" he muttered.

Quite alarmed now, Harry went through the house, checking for disturbances and turning on all the lights. His house shone out like a small football stadium. He even checked to see if the radio in the kitchen was switched off. Under an impulse, he turned it on to be greeted by some cacophonous crap that masqueraded as music. He twitched the dial and reached a night-time phone-in programme. "I'd just like to know if anyone else out there has seen aliens slinking about in their garden at night?" the caller was asking. His doom-laden voice was deep and croaky, betraying a forty-a-day smoker. He rambled on about some seriously abstruse theory that was, predictably, all his own work.

"Ye gods! The nutters of the night. That's all I need," Harry said. "He's enough to make me want to piss off to Pluto." He wondered if the caller might get kidnapped by the skulking aliens in his shrubbery and thereby give humanity a chance, then whispered, "Probably no such fucking luck."

Satisfied that windows and doors were still secure, he went back to the bedroom. Harry tiptoed toward the paintings and then, hesitantly, straightened them. Suspending his disbelief, he put it down to a sudden baffling draught — perhaps wind gusting down the chimney. Still, even with this explanation, a creepy 'not alone' feeling crawled up his spine and made its way, steady as a march of ants, to his neck. He spun round, frightened. "Get a grip, man!" he chided himself.

Harry got back into bed after climbing into a clean set of pyjamas and propped himself up. He wasn't going to sleep tonight. The wind and rain were still engulfing the house. Nameless things banged in the street, and he heard a roof tile crash nearby. Harry remembered the newspaper story of the famous hurricane in the eighties. A huge piece of thick plastic had taken flight from a flat roof and hit a chimney at colossal speed, bringing it down into a bloke's bedroom where he was getting over the flu. Had it hit him, his recovery would have been pointless. After, what seemed like hours, Harry dozed off, despite the meteorological turmoil outside.

His slumber was short. A furious exchange started up again, and in astonishment, he fell from his bed. He got up and stared across the room to where the voices emanated. "The fucking things are talking to each other!" he cried aloud in shock and fear. Every nerve ending on his head tingled. With a scream, he fled the room, smashing into the door jamb in his panic, giving himself a huge blow to the chin, which dislodged two teeth. He careered madly to the top of the stairs, and in his wild haste to get out of the house, tripped. Harry fell headlong, tumbling over and over, finally hitting the landing with an ominous crash.

Harry was discovered some days later, as a neighbour reported all the lights on day and night and thought it warranted investigation. Harry was found at the bottom of the stairs in a heap, his neck clearly broken as his head was almost looking behind him. His pyjamas were round his ankles, revealing his nakedness. He looked rather ridiculous.

Part Three

David, Harry's son, came to make the necessary arrangements for the funeral and see that his late father's affairs were up to date. While looking through his dad's various papers, he came across the receipt for the two panel paintings in his father's bedroom. Now, David took a particular interest in this because he had been to art school. He was intrigued that such paintings cost so little. Therefore, after a few days, he searched for the shop, taking the elaborate receipt with him. David had no clear idea of why he wanted to do this. He had a vague notion that the paintings were quite valuable, but their price was ludicrous. He felt, also, a strange presence around them, and it made him jittery. David found the lane and turned into it. At first, he thought it was the wrong lane, as there was no shop at the number on the receipt; well, there was, but not a bookshop. David found himself looking into a small 7/11 supermarket. He walked about searching, but nothing. David thought this really odd and asked about, but no one remembered a shop anything like the one he described. Seemingly, it had vanished.

That night, as David slept in the spare room, he thought he could hear people arguing, probably just outside the street. *It seemed like a bitter argument,* he thought, through his sleepy haze.

Part Four

Now that the funeral was over, David contacted a classy firm of art auctioneers to get some idea of the worth of the two paintings. Two days later, he was in the office of a London firm laying the two portraits out on a large mahogany table. Two experts were in attendance, and both admired the quality of the work: its colour, details, and the expert rendering. David left them with the auctioneers so they could do some research, and he went back to Brighton to conclude his father's affairs. Some days later, he received a call from the company asking him to come back up to London. David went again in the afternoon of the next day, but no wiser than before, as the auctioneer said he wanted to talk to David in person.

David reached the office about 4:00 p.m. and was, to his amazement, shown straight into a plush room. It was quite a step up from his first visit and encouraged, he sat in a large Chesterfield. Someone brought him coffee and a selection of biscuits.

The door opened after a few minutes, and two rather posh figures strode into the room. These were not the men he saw previously. They introduced themselves as senior partners. David's heart was thudding now as he smelt money.

"Well, Mr. Fielding, we have a fascinating story for you and an offer we hope you will consider most seriously." It was the taller of the two who spoke first. His voice was mellow and well-practiced, something between a solicitor and a lounge-lizard. He was also quite swarthy. David thought he would be the one who would conduct whatever negotiations they were starting.

"Very interesting, indeed. We've tracked down who these two people are — and in quite some detail, too," the other added. In looks, he was clearly the more pleasure-seeking of the two: fully-girthed with sensual red lips that could do justice to Botox. *A premiere league two-fisted drinker*, David thought.

"Firstly, be assured we're delighted to tell you, Mr. Fielding, that they are late fifteenth-century Italians." The taller confirmed this with a wide smile and gleaming teeth.

"Florentine actually, unsurprisingly." The shorter now. David wondered if they were some kind of regular double act at these gigs.

This thought was confirmed when his partner went on to explain, "What you have here, Mr. Fielding, are portraits of Jacopo de' Pazzi." He held up one of the small pictures in a white-gloved hand, "and here, Piero di Cosimo de' Medici called 'The Gouty.' Both were noble Florentines in the *quattrocento*, and both were heads of their respective family. However, Piero had died earlier in 1469, and the succession went to his eldest son, Lorenzo. Lorenzo sported the appellation 'The Magnificent.'"

"Eh? The quat-what?" David queried.

"Fourteen hundreds, Mr. Fielding. The fourteen hundreds." Again, it was an interjection by the florid, venal one.

"What you have here, Mr. Fielding, are two rival members of the most powerful families in Florence, a piece of history relating to the Congiura dai Pazzi or Pazzi Conspiracy. And a gory one it was, Mr. Fielding, with much high drama and bloodshed!" David's eyes widened, more because he could see pound signs and hear the ring of a till.

"Now imagine the scene, Mr. Fielding: it is Easter Sunday, and High Mass is being chanted in Florence's Santa Maria delle Fiore cathedral. A crowd of around ten thousand has gathered outside, and all the nobles of Florence are inside. Sacred music and swirling incense. But in this sacred space, an assignation plot to kill Lorenzo and his brother is about to unfold.

"At the elevation of the host, Lorenzo's brother, Giuliano de' Medici, is suddenly set upon by Francesco de' Pazzi and his friend Bernardo Bandini dei Baroncelli and savagely murdered. A skull-splitting blow from a sword strikes him, and he is stabbed some nineteen times in the chest. Worshipers fall back in horror as blood spurts from Giuliano's brain and heart. Francesco's blood-lust is so fierce he even stabs himself in the leg.

"As Giuliano bleeds to death on the cathedral's marble floor, Lorenzo is attacked; two priests who were coerced into the plot grab him from behind. Lorenzo is standing up by the high altar, and the priests being unschooled in the art of assassination fail to make a lethal strike. Despite receiving a stab wound in the neck, he escapes to the sacristy with the aid of his friend Angelo Ambrogini — better known by his nickname Poliziano."

The other partner took over the narrative: "High drama indeed, Mr. Fielding. Many famous co-plotters lent help, but principally it was Pope Sixtus IV, Francisco Salviati the Archbishop of Pisa, and the famous condottiere Federico da Montefeltro with his six hundred men who were to

90

secure the city when the brothers had been killed.

"A coordinated attempt to capture the Gonfaloniere and the Signoria — rather like our Mayor and Council — was thwarted when the archbishop and head of the Salviati clan were trapped in a room where the doors were held by a hidden latch. Jacopo de' Pazzi went to the Pizza Vecchio to persuade the crowds to support the coup, but with mixed success; worse, the Papal-supported troops didn't arrive, and without the capture of the Signoria and lockdown of the city, the plot then ultimately failed." His voice trailed to a soft dramatic whisper.

David sat transfixed at the story and super-transfixed at what this might do to up his financial rewards.

"Now, imagine the fear of the Pazzi and their co-conspirators," the other continued. "Bloodshed and revenge follow: the Piazza Vecchio becomes a theatre of grim reckoning. With popular outrage and family retribution, corpses of the guilty soon lay about the city. Over the next few days, the Pazzi family are executed or exiled. Others are beaten and mutilated. Francesco de' Pazzi is hanged from the third window of the Loggia dei Lanzi along with Archbishop Salviati. Old Jacopo de' Pazzi and the priest conspirators suffer the same fate. Bernardo Baroncelli flees to Constantinople, but later is captured and returned in fetters for execution. In all, over eighty conspirators died.

"The Pazzi name was then expunged from Florence, Mr. Fielding — the dolphin arms of the family chiselled off stone, and street names changed. Anyone bearing the Pazzi name was made to change it; anyone married into the Pazzi was barred from public office."

The relator looked at David and could see he was fully engaged in the narrative. David thought this was the time to cut to the chase.

"That's quite a backstory! So, this must make them quite valuable works of art then? If, and I say if, I wanted to sell them, that is." David intended to play this close to his chest.

"Oh, indeed, Mr. Fielding!" the two partners said almost in unison. David had an image of Tweedledum and Tweedledee.

"At auction, they could raise many thousands each. But there again, maybe not. It can be quite uncertain. You may not even get your reserve. Can be difficult," said the corpulent partner. "Which is why we want you to consider selling the pictures in a private sale. Mr. Westerman here is prepared to offer you a substantial sum to have them in his collection at home." He indicated his tall business partner.

"Large sum, you say?" David found it hard to enunciate as he had a parched mouth now.

"A million pounds. In cash." David realised that it was the corpulent guy conducting the details of this negotiation. He'd gotten it all wrong.

"You see, Mr. Fielding, I would love to have them. Really, I would!" Mr. Westerman cried. "I have a particular interest in Florentine history, which explains the large sum I am prepared to pay. My offer is a very good one, sir."

David was wondering if he could talk the price up, but he was young and inexperienced in these things. The thought of a million pounds was too tempting to mess up by being greedy. David accepted the deal. Mr. Westerman had a private bill-of-sale already prepared and took David's bank details. Within fifteen minutes, David was able to confirm the transfer, and "as happy as Larry," he left the offices.

Novis finis.

Mr. Westerman had fallen asleep on the sofa in his living room. It was well after twelve o'clock, and the lighting was dim; he could just make out the two newly acquired portraits he was so pleased to have. He let out a sigh of happiness. Then his blood ran cold; the screams and accusations of murder rang round the room.

The End

Captain's Log
by
Colleen M. Farrelly

March 25, 2525
Sanibee FOB, Alpha*11

Faz shot down a Wapaxi recon ship today. I performed an ultra-high altitude, high opening jump to administer the cauterization laser and reconstructive gel, per section 3.11B protocol under which enemy are resuscitated and taken as prisoners of war for intelligence purposes. It was too late, though.

last laugh —
impaled by
a life support pack

Jexa is still not returning my holotexts. I fear she may never speak to me again after volunteering for this post. Hopefully, the outpost garden's roses don't turn black in her matter reconstructor again. Of all the planets in all the galaxies, she had to land on mine…

methane clouds
veiling the twin suns —
relationships

The men are asleep as I keep watch tonight. So far, all is quiet on the Kuiper Belt.
The End

Where the Stars Light Out
by
Christopher Dabrowski

They didn't expect this. They would rather think they would see God, but this was way beyond their mental abilities. Suddenly, all theories about parallel universes found a logical explanation. All theses telling that a dying space is replaced by a new one also proved correct! Captain Hans Olo looked back at his crew. Everyone was moved; they couldn't believe their eyes. No one expected to see...

****

Did the descendants have a moral right to decide for the future generations? Did the mission justify the fact that Earth became a myth (an old, dusty myth that must be known because it is your duty) for them?

For over three thousand years, Manta Saria, a giant spaceship, roamed the cosmic emptiness to accomplish something that would once have been pure madness. Centuries ago, scientists proved that the universe ends at a certain spot. A few centuries later, they showed that the end was material, as if a giant wall surrounded everything. Ever since, they believed that it was of the highest importance to check what could be found behind the end. Some even called the expedition "To discover God." Soon the jokes would become a prophecy.

They passed many galaxies. When one of them looked promising in terms of existence of life, or at least had a planet where people could set up a colony, they immediately sent research probes. Despite the lack of success, they could afford to be wasteful. Thanks to nanotechnology, the vehicles were built of a mere thousand atoms.

Three thousand years in the black emptiness. Over twenty generations that knew Earth only from their textbooks. They sometimes asked themselves whether it all made sense or if they were heading for their own doom. Did they have the right to see the face of God? To prove the existence of the Highest One, if he was there?

For over fifty years, Hans Olo was the leader of the expedition, and there was not a single day when he was not haunted by these questions without answers.

They planned the most important escapade in the humankind era in the finest details. In the preparation phase, the toughest problem was food production. To keep the crew alive, they would have to have the storage area one hundred times larger than the whole ship. It took a few years to invent a molecular generator and to save the whole project. The device would degrade waste to atoms and create anything from those atoms, including food. Salvation and curse, at the same time. Curse, because nothing could be wasted – even the dead and the feces were degraded to atoms and then eaten in a form of generated food. They never knew the taste of real, Earth-made food like juicy fruit, bloody steaks. Everything they produced had a similar, slightly paper-like taste.

Although he spent his whole life here and he knew no other food, the thought of the deceased turned to food raised a non-determined, primal feeling of disgust and fear. The fact that his body digested processed feces was somehow acceptable, but the fact that maybe one day he ate his parents...

Fuel was a lot less troublesome. There was doubt that lightspeed could be surpassed. However, due to the use of antimatter as fuel and invention of new, extremely damage-resistant materials, engineers managed to obtain sub-light speed only slightly slower than that achieved by photons.

Despite undisputable success, scientists were still in despair. It would take the ship over a million years to reach its destination. Preparations got stuck in a dead point for ten years. Every day, fewer people believed that the project would be successful. Some voices of outrage could be heard because the planetary government spent many billions of eurolars, which of course was the biggest burden for the poorest taxpayers. They didn't care about some expeditions; they were cosmic extravagances.

One night, soaked with resignation, one of the very young astrophysicists rose to his feet from his bed and until morning, with madness in his eyes, calculated formulas that he had dreamt of. He created a theory of time-space curve synchronization. To put it as simply as can be, the youngster managed to create "a road map of the universe" and to create "tunnels" in the space-time curves. In practice, this meant that getting to the destination point would take almost three thousand years, which was acceptable.

When the spaceship was almost built, the greatest minds of both sexes were gathered together. Among them, five thousand volunteers were selected; half were men, half women. The chosen ones had to accept just one condition: they had to make pairs, and each pair had to have two children. This cycle had to be repeated for many future generations. Generations that had no choice.

Then, day 0 came! For five thousand brave men and women, the time started a new cycle. Just like long before the birth of Jesus marked the beginning, now the launch of Manta Saria was the new start. The chosen representatives of humankind embarked on a volunteer mission. It was a sacrifice that would be incorporated into the academic curriculum forever, regardless of the result.

Hans often wondered what Earth looked like now. He was born among the stars, not on a remote, blue planet, but he missed it strangely as if deep in his genes, a bond with this primal mother of humankind was encoded. True, they received news via information beam, but the transmissions were distorted due to different radiation types and curves of the time-space. They were also outdated, unfortunately. All news was two thousand years late. Most probably, no one would ever solve the problem of communication over such distances. This was still better than nothing. The Earth might not exist anymore, and they would learn about it in two thousand years.

Most probably, he was not the only one to have thoughts like that. The whole crew was born on the ship in space, and they would also most probably die in the black depth. Still, everyone had to know the culture, history and geography of their ancestor's home planet. And all this just to teach the future generations, to keep the memory of Earth. After all, their descendants would return there one day.

The longer they flew, the more suspicious the theories became. Someone said that they were escaping, and that the blue planet was invaded by aliens. Someone insisted that they had no place to return to since the mother planet collided with a giant meteoroid. One person even invented such a curious theory that Earth never existed. The ship was there always since the beginning of time! This made the hair rise on Hans's head! The best, most meticulously chosen genes of geniuses created the children, and there was such madness in their heads! Luckily for them, they were almost at their destination point.

A sudden shake and pulses of bass vibrations woke him from his thoughts. They were decelerating. For the first time in a few years their speed was decreasing. They had reached their target! It was just a mere thousand kilometers to the "end of the universe." They would meet the unknown in a bit more than an hour. The sensors were going mad, squeaking to alert the crew about a huge obstacle made of unidentified matter. Hans turned the alerts off. The crew needed silence and concentration. This was an extraordinary moment. They couldn't make the slightest error.

Manta Saria approached its destination steadily, left behind the space that sparkled with quadrillions of galaxies and aimed at the ideal blackness. The order forces and emergency services were ready. Commandos took their positions at the blasters and military vehicles. On every level, there was chaos. People crowded in front of giant screens transmitting the whole action and the speech of the leader. Their faces showed different emotions from fear to excitement. Maybe these were the last moments of their lives, or maybe this was their ticket to a new, better universe.

For almost all of his life, Hans Olo had prepared for this very moment. He had imagined it a million times; it even invaded his dreams. When it finally came true, he could not hold his emotions in. His voice trembled, his heart pounded, and sweat flowed in abundant rivers over his gray hair.

The crew could not see their leader in such a condition. He decided to send his deputy to read his speech on his behalf.

Next, his most important task was to compare the latest data. They could analyze the barrier thoroughly since they were so close to it.

Scientists rushed nervously around the research instruments, and they reviewed hundreds of printouts. Another ten, up to fifteen, minutes and he would call everyone to get a detailed report. They would have a real brainstorm.

The ship stopped a kilometer away from the end. A miniaturized research nanoprobe launched. It shot out at an enormous speed to suddenly stop a mere meter from the unknown matter. In the blink of an eye, it started transmitting detailed data recorded by the sensors, getting ready at the same time to go through the intermolecular gaps of the barrier.

This was no brainstorm; it was a real tornado. Eventually, decisions about future actions had to be made based on information sent from the nanoprobe after it penetrated to the other side of the barrier. Everyone had their eyes fixed on the screens. At the beginning, everything was dark, but then it became lighter. Finally, they saw a blinding whiteness. The computers printed new portions of data. One of the scientists approached Hans, holding a printout as if it was a million eurolars voucher. He almost exploded with emotions for what felt like an eternity. He could not make any sound. Finally, he shouted out in a trembling voice:

"There is an atmosphere over there!"

Analyses and live discussions lasted for a few hours. Finally, they decided that they had to cross the barrier to get to the other side. The risk of something unexpected was enormous, but so many generations gave their lives away from the Earth that they couldn't do anything else. Because there was an atmosphere on the other side, they decided to surround Manta Saria with a bubble of dark matter plasma. As soon as the construct stuck to the barrier, it started to drill through it. In the fly-through point, they generated a time-space loop to prevent anything from the other universe from migrating to where it shouldn't go. Even if some of the atmosphere got through, it would get stuck in the loop forever without any damage.

After a few, stressful hours, they arrived at the unknown universe. Most of the cameras momentarily focused on the barrier so that they could see what it looked like on the other side. It was light pink, rough and… It started to move away very quickly at a speed so unbelievable that the research instruments protested since they lacked scale. The terrified crew froze.

The further away their universe, the more it resembled a shape of a child. Their space was just a cell in a giant organism. It was part of a few-year-old, unsuspecting kid. Was the universe of this child also just a cell, one of many billions, in somebody else's body? Did he also have a universe in each of his cells? Hans felt that he would go mad at any moment. Even now, biting his lips until they bled, was he killing billions of creatures, destroying their universes?

He saw sudden darkness in front of his eyes.

He fainted.

The End

About the Contributors

Linda Barrett:

Ms. Barrett has been writing all her life. She wrote her first book at the age of eight. It's still in the McKinley Elementary school library. She was published in the *Huntingdon Junior Library* literary magazine by age thirteen. She's won three awards with the Montgomery County Community College Writer's contest. "Mr. Cat's Revenge" won third place in the 2014 MCCC contest. Ms. Barrett lives with her 84 years young mother in Abington in the same house for 50 years.

Rajeev Bhargava:

Rajeev lives in Harrow with his parents and five Chihuahuas. He has been writing since the age of twelve but had his first work published in 1990. Since then he's been writing stories, poems and articles for the small press as well as mainstream. His ambition is to be a freelance writer.

S. M. Bidwell:

Sharon writes multi-genre now under three variations of her name. Given free rein, she veers to the disturbing with an undercurrent of the mysterious or unpleasant. The ability to write twisted tales has led to appearances in many publications. Longer works most notably include *Space: 1889*, and *Doctor Who* related fiction. Now living in the south-west of England, she hopes to write more stories that are dark, and gritty. She has lived in a house with a Harry Potter cupboard under the stairs, shared a publisher with the creator of *Roger Rabbit*, and once took a trip to Jupiter. Only one of these has been in her imagination. http://www.sharonbidwell.co.uk

Francis-Marie de Châtillon:

Professional art historian and university lecturer. In a long-term domestic partnership with an NHS midwife. Lives in London and Florence. Lived in Brazil and Spain. New to fiction writing. On Facebook.

Ron J. Cruz:

Ron Cruz breathes and pens fiction in a house set upon an abandoned goldmine in the foothills below the Sierra Nevada Mountain Range in California. He earned a Master's Degree in literature from California State University Sacramento where he won the Bazanella Literary Award for fiction. Currently Cruz teaches English composition at Sierra and Folsom Lake College. His writing has appeared in a number of publications such as "Sanitarium", "69 Flavors of Paranoia," "Not One of Us, "Literary Orphans", "Surreal Grotesque", and "Bewildering Stories." For more information on Ron J. Cruz, check out www.ronjcruz.com

Christopher T. Dabrowski:

Christopher has had numerous books published in the USA and Poland. His USA works include: *Anomaly* and *Escape*, both published by the Royal Hawaiian Press. Books published in Poland include *Anima Vilis* (Initium), *Grobbing* (Novae Res), *Deathbirth and other Stories* (Agharta & Amoryka), *Orgazmokalipsa* (Alternatywne publishing house), *Anomalia* (Forma publishing house), and *Ucieczka* (2017 - Dom Horroru publishing house). Monika Olasek provided the English translation for his *Night to Dawn* stories.

Sandy DeLuca:

Sandy has written five novels; *Settling in Nazareth* (she painted the cover art), *Descent, Manhattan Grimoire, From Ashes,* and *Requiem for the Dead.* Her poetry chapbook, *Burial Plot in Sagittarius* (also created cover art and illustrations), was nominated for the BRAM STOKER award in 2001. Her art has been exhibited in galleries, hair salons, book stores and online venues. She has also painted covers and contributed interior illustrations for various numerous small press venues.

David Ennocenti:

David Ennocenti is a graduate of The University of Buffalo. His many letters to the editor have appeared in the *New York Times, USA Today,* and several other publications. He placed eighth in *The Writer's Digest* Annual Competition. His screenplay *Sniper Queen* was an official selection in The Artemis Women in Action Films Festival. At the present time, he is in the process of writing a sitcom and developing a drama series based on "Blood on the Hill." He lives in Rochester, New York.

Colleen M. Farrelly:

Colleen M. Farrelly is a freelance writer living in Miami, FL, whose haibun have recently appeared in *Frogpond, Haibun Today, Contemporary Haibun Online, the other bunny, cattails, Scifaikuest,* and many others. She is a machine learning scientist by day and is working on a machine learning textbook through *No Starch Press.*

Chris Friend:

Chris has published his art in small press horror magazines for nearly 25 years. His surreal horror images have been featured in *Stygian Articles, Realm of the Vampire, Deathrealm, Black Petals,* and *Space and Time.* He draws his inspiration from Harry Clarke, H. R. Giger, and the horror comics of the 70s such as the Tomb of Dracula her and the Hammer Studios Frankenstein films. Chris friend can be reached at Mars_art_13@yahoo.com. Chris friend can be reached at Mars_art_13@yahoo.com.

To sample his illustrations, go to http://chris.michaelherring.net and http://www.moonlit-path.com/art-2-13-06.htm.

Todd Hanks:

The creative writing of Todd Hanks has been seen in publications such as Asimov's Science Fiction Magazine and the Kansas City Star newspaper.

Teresa Jay:

Originating from the UK but now residing in the Canary Islands, freelance artist Teresa Tunaley finds more time to devote to her love of art and painting. For years she has been doodling with pencils and dabbling with watercolors. More recently she uses a more modern technique and creates with her electronic tablet and pen in software such as Photoshop, Corel Draw and Paint Shop Pro. Along with published stories and poetry, she can be credited with award winning cover art and illustrations for author stories. Her work can be seen online and in print across the UK, US, Canada, Denmark and Europe. As Teresa put it, "I would like to think that I am very versatile in my choice of subject matter – my new surroundings provide the inspiration for me to paint on a daily basis and the fact that others may enjoy my work gives me the confidence to continue."

Website portfolio https://teresatunaley.wixsite.com/artstopper; E-mail post@artstopper.com

Tom Johnson:

Tom, a Vietnam veteran with twenty years in the military police (L.E.), has enjoyed literary success as a science fiction novelist with his action adventures in the Jurassic Period of Earth's predawn. He has created short story SF characters like Captain Danger of the *Space Rangers* and the galactic master thief, *The Forever Man* as futuristic space opera adventure. His many costumed crime fighters include two of his own creations, such as *The Black Ghost* and *The Masked Avenger,* as well as a western masked hero of the plains called *The Nightwind.* He has upcoming stories of *Ki-Gor the Jungle Lord,* and Greek heroes like Hercules and Atalanta. For the latest information on Tom and his writing, check out his websites:

http://www15.brinkster.com/jur1/index.html
www.geocities.com/fadingshadows1/index.html.

Rod Marsden:

Rod Marsden hails from Sydney, Australia. He has three degrees related to writing and history. His stories have been published in Australia, England, Russia, the USA and now Canada. He has work in the American anthology *Cats Do it Better,* the American steam punkanthology *Break Time* and in the Canadian anthology *Morbid Metamorphosis.* Many of his short stories have been published in *Night to Dawn* magazine. His books include *Undead Reb Down Under and Other Vampire Stories, Disco Evil: Dead Man's Stand, Ghost Dance,* and *Desk Job* (his salute to Lewis Carroll). *Cold Water Conscience* is his venture into Crime/Horror. His short play, *Zombie Vision,* was well received at Cronulla Arts Theatre. His play *Hyde and Seek* was even better received. Rod has a fondness for Cronulla and the Wollongong area but an abiding love for the more northern Clarence River region of his home state of New South Wales.

Denny E. Marshall:

Denny E. Marshall has had art, poetry, and fiction published. Some recent credits include interior art in *Midnight Echo #14* Dec. 2019, cover art for *Society Of Misfit Stories* Feb. 2020, and poetry in *Space & Time Magazine #134* Fall 2019. This year his website is celebrating 20 years on the web. Also in 2020 his artwork is for sale for the first time. It is available on Zazzle as posters coffee cups, puzzles, mouse pads, etc. The link is on his website. (Click on top left drawing.) See more at www.dennymarshall.com.

James Masters:

James was born in Tampa, Florida. When he was 16, his father died in an auto accident. This led to him moving to Ohio, and eventually, Parkersburg, West Virginia. He now works in Security and illustrates fantasy. He's been sketching since an early age and plans to send more illustrations to be featured in Night to Dawn.

Elizabeth Hattie Pierce-Collins:

Elizabeth first learned art and drawing from her mother. From there, she was self-taught until she was able to attend art school. She loves drawing the human figure and never stops studying the human body in motion. Her illustrations have appeared in *Night to Dawn* magazine and *The Spider's Web* (a novel). These have drawn positive attention from the readers. Elizabeth hopes to appear in more magazines and books in the future. For more information, contact Elizabeth at wackyursalinan45@aol.com.

Marge Simon:

Marge Simon's works appear in publications such as DailySF Magazine, Pedestal, Dreams& Nightmares. She edits a column for the HWA Newsletter, "Blood & Spades: Poets of the Dark Side," and serves as Chair of the Board of Trustees. She won the Strange Horizons Readers Choice Award, 2010, and the SFPA's Dwarf Stars Award, 2012. She has won three Bram Stoker Awards ® for Superior Work in Poetry, two first place Rhysling Awards and the Grand Master Award from the SF Poetry Association, 2015. In addition to her poetry, she has published two prose collections: *Christina's World*, Sam's Dot Publications, 2008 and *Like Birds in the Rain*, Sam's Dot, 2007. Her poems appear in *Qualia Nous* (Written Backwards), *The Dark Phantastique* (Jasunni Productions), Spectral Realms anthologies by S.T. Joshi, and more poems will appear in *Chiral Mad 3* and *Scary Out There*, a HWA/ Simon & Schuster Y/A collection, 2015. www.margesimon.com

Marc Shapiro:

When not contributing short stories and poetry to the small press, Marc Shapiro moonlights as the author of unauthorized celebrity biographies. Coming soon is *Keanu Reeves Excellent Adventure*. He has also penned the life and times of such big names as Lynn Manuel Miranda, Donald Trump, Greta Van Fleet, and the Korean boy band BTS.

Matias Travieso-Diaz:

Matias is a lawyer. He retired recently after four decades of practice, during which he generated a large number of writings, including two books and many published articles, which were well received by critics and the public. After his retirement, he redirected his efforts towards creative writing and authored a number of stories of various lengths and genres (one of his stories was published in *March in the New Reader Magazine*). The enclosed unpublished story, "The Satchel" (2,970 words), is representative of his dark speculative fiction.

Matthew Wilson:

Matthew Wilson has had over 150 appearances in such places as *Horror Zine, Star*Line, Spellbound, Illumen, Apokrupha Press, Gaslight Press, Sorcerers Signal* and many more. He is currently editing his first novel and can be contacted on twitter @matthew94544267.

Lee Clark Zumpe:

Lee Clark Zumpe has been writing and publishing horror, dark fantasy and speculative fiction since the late 1990s. His short stories and poetry have appeared in a variety of publications such as *Weird Tales, Space and Time* and *Dark Wisdom;* and in anthologies such as *Dark Horizons, Best New Zombie Tales Vol. 3, Dread Shadows in Paradise, Heroes of Red Hook* and *World War Cthulhu*. His work has earned several honorable mentions in *The Year's Best Fantasy and Horror* collections.

An entertainment columnist with Tampa Bay Newspapers, Lee has penned hundreds of film, theater and book reviews and has interviewed novelists as well as music industry icons such as Paddy Moloney of The Chieftains and Alan Parsons. His work for TBN has been recognized repeatedly by the Florida Press Association, including a first-place award for criticism in the 2013 Better Weekly Newspaper Contest.

Lee lives on the west coast of Florida with his wife and daughter. Visit www.leeclarkzumpe.com.